Ladies' Man

Elbow Chronicles, Volume 1

Kay Wahlgren

Published by Kay Wahlgren, 2022.

LADIES' MAN

First edition. August 24, 2022.

ISBN: 979-8230688242

Written by Kay Wahlgren.

Table of Contents

To Ron and Christine Edison and Writers@Work DuPage

As the dinner plates started flying in his direction, 'Elbow' ran for the safety of the rowboat pulled up on the spit of gravel near the scrub palms at the river's edge. Stupid woman! She never did understand the finer points of give and take in a relationship.

He made it to the rowboat with only minor damage to his ego or his head. As he dragged the aging boat into the muddy water, two dessert plates zinged past his ear and skipped several times on the water surface. Damn, she was a good shot. Better hurry before she remembered there was a shotgun in the bedroom closet.

The old wooden boat launched heavily into the moving current. He suddenly realized it would carry him closer to the pier and the house. He pulled frantically at the cord on the ancient outboard motor. It made a few anemic ticks, then stood frozen in all its crusty, Evinrude majesty on the back of the boat. The smell of leaking gasoline hung heavily in the air as an oily swirl spread out into the water. Damn! Damn, damn!

He glanced at the house. She was gone from the doorway. She remembered the gun. Damn! Nothing left to do now but row. Oars! Where were the damn oars?! He looked at the rapidly retreating riverbank. The oars were neatly placed against a palm tree, almost laughing at him.

He stood up and urgently clawed his way to the front of the boat, carelessly rocking the boat from side to side. His knee caught a protruding nail on the right gunwale. It tore his jeans and sent him sprawling into the foul smelling, gray liquid in the bottom of the boat. Fish scales! He ignored the blood trickling down his leg and made a final push to the bow of the boat. Lying flat against the bow he reached down into the river and paddled with all his might. Miraculously, the boat missed the pier and moved away into the fast, middle current. He breathed a sigh of relief.

BLAM! The blast of the shotgun caught the outboard motor, sending shrapnel cascading down on him.

He stood up. "You're crazy, you know that! Crazy!"

BLAM! Another shot echoed out across the water, this time hitting the boat just above the water line. The shot was deliberate. She was too good a shot. She was trying to sink it,

He paddled again with increasing urgency. The swirling current turned the boat in the opposite direction taking it farther down stream. He looked up. He could see her on the pier, reloading.

He paddled backwards, trying to adjust to the turning motion of the boat to put more space between him and the shotgun. He saw her take aim. He pushed himself down into the filthy water in the bottom of the boat.

BLAM! BLAM! Two shots. The first one blasted a nasty hole in the gunwale right above his head. The second hit the motor again, and this time gasoline and oil sprayed out into the boat. He stayed where he was, huddled in a fetal position, covered with gasoline, oil, wood splinters and fish goo. Maybe she would think she got him and quit the barrage.

After several moments he dared lift his head to peak over the gunwale. The current had carried the boat around the bend in the river and unless she came after him in another boat, he was safe, at least for now.

The first shotgun blast had done a number on the front of the boat at the water line. Water was steadily seeping in through the damaged boards. He stood up and clamored to the back of the boat to try to tip the front above the leak.

His knee stung like a hundred furries as gasoline found its way into the wound. Blood from his leg mixed with the muddy mess at the bottom of the boat. That's going to need stitches.

Man, that woman was mean. It was all a misunderstanding. How was he supposed to know she wanted to get serious. She could have at

least given him a clue so he could have made his exit sooner instead of springing it on him all at once. And then when he hemmed and hawed a little, like any respectable dude, she got all uptight and started throwing plates at him. She could have been sporting and given him a running start. He rubbed his jaw where one of the plates clipped it. At least this time he still had all his teeth.

Louisa was a beaut though. With those long lashes and those curves, she could sigh and half the men in the county would have crawled on the ground to hear to it. Her only major flaw was her husband, Big Joe. Women! You could never predict when they were going to turn on you. One minute they were all lovey-dovey-sweety-pie and the next thing they're slinging plates and running for shotguns.

He lay back in the boat, closed his eyes and let the current take the boat farther down river. The day promised to be as humid as any other in the everglades as the sun rose higher in the sky. Might as well enjoy it, at least until the afternoon thunderstorms got organized and dumped more water in the river.

The boat drifted lazily from sun to the dappled shade of cypress trees as it turned in the currant. He could smell the sweet, smokey aroma of barbecue somewhere down river. Arnie's Bar and Grill. It had its own, unmistakable fragrance, a bit of honey-spice barbecue mixed with cigarette smoke.

He sat up. The boat was taking on some serious water. If he could make it to Arnie's, he was home free. He wasn't exactly a river man. He had no idea where he really was on the river. Arnie's could be around the next bend or several miles of twists and turns away, but the smell of barbecue was getting more intense.

The sluggish, water-filled boat bumped into roots on the riverbank. Elbow swung his leg over the side to push it off a cypress root. His injured knee hung out of the torn jeans. It was a gritty mess. The sting had subsided to a dull throb. Gotta get that looked at, he thought.

The side current caught the boat again and slowly pushed it around the next bend in the river. Arnie's! There it was on the opposite riverbank. If he didn't move fast, the current was going to take the boat right past the pier and around the next bend. He scrambled toward the front of the boat and started flaying the water furiously to steer it to the opposite shore. Full of water now, the boat was as heavy as an anchor.

Elbow beat the water with all his might, his arms turning like windmills, sending a froth of water into the air. He tried to will the uncooperative boat to turn and head for Arnie's pier. Progress was slow. Damn boat. "Move!" he yelled.

On the riverbank, a large, greenish log moved slightly in the water. Two ancient, yellow eyes opened and studied the fountain of water erupting in the middle of the river, then disappeared silently below the surface.

Elbow wasn't even looking where he was going, just pummeling the water in a desperate effort to make it to Arnie's pier before the boat sank or the current carried it away. Bonk! His head collided with one of the pier posts. He grabbed on and hugged it for dear life. He made it. Now he was safe.

"What you doing in my boat," said a deep voice above him on the pier.

Elbow winced. Damn. It was Big Joe, Louisa's husband, all 300 surly pounds of him. Elbow put on his friendliest grin. "It's kind of a complicated story, Big Joe. Help me out of this thing and I'll buy you a beer and tell you about it." If Big Joe didn't kill him immediately, buying him a beer would at least allow a few minutes to think up a good story. Big Joe grunted and reached down into the boat with his meaty paw to haul Elbow up onto the pier.

"Thanks, Big Joe," Elbow told him with relief. His skinny knees gave out under him and he sat down on the rickety pier.

Big Joe laughed with a low rumbling sound. "Yeah, it'd be a shame if the gator got you."

Elbow looked in the water behind the boat just as a giant tail thrashed and hit the stern.

BLAM! BLAM! Big Joe pulled off two shots into the water with his hand gun. "Missed," he said as he stuffed the gun back in his belt.

Elbow swallowed hard. How long had that thing been following him with that leaky boat trailing a tempting flow of fish scales and blood behind him? "Thanks again, Big Joe." Elbow's voice squeaked. He managed a weak smile and crawled over to one of the pier pilings to raise himself up, not at all sure if his legs would cooperate enough to stand.

"You said somethin' bout a beer?"

"Yeah, Big Joe, just let me get my land legs under me and we'll have a cold one."

Elbow limped a little, trailing wet, bloody footprints behind him as they walked the length of the pier and the raised, plank walkway up to Arnie's porch. The whole establishment was set on stilts to accommodate the fickle levels of the river. Sometimes the water left

it high and dry and sometimes it lapped at the underside of the floorboards. Wet or dry, Arnie's neon sign on the roof was always on and it was open to thirsty customers.

Elbow took in the dark and soothing atmosphere of Arnie's inner sanctum. Something about the black, nicotine-stained walls and glitter of the bottles in front of the fly-specked mirror said home to him. The bug zapper hummed away on the porch and a rigged video game flashed its monotonous colored lights in the corner.

And then there was Wanda. Today she was looking particularly fine with her black hair pulled back and a red flower behind her ear. A little past her prime but still in possession of a few ample feminine attributes, she was a fixture behind the bar. Her husband, Arnie, welcomed admiring glances at his wife, it encouraged more trips to the bar, but it was strictly look-but-don't-touch. A few unlucky souls had tested the house rule and felt Arnie's displeasure. It didn't bother Wanda. She was always there, ready to chat up anyone who wanted to admire.

"Well, if it isn't Elbow. What'll it be, honey?"

"Two beers, Wanda, cold ones."

"Sure thing. You look like you got yourself in a tangle. You're drippin' blood all over my nice clean floor."

The floor hadn't been cleaned since the last hurricane flooded the place and carted off the top layer of grunge, but Elbow apologized just to be polite. "Sorry, Wanda, its been a hell of a morning."

"You just sit yourself down. Two beers coming up. I'll fetch somethin' to fix that nasty scratch on your knee."

Big Joe settled himself heavily in the metal chair at the table facing the doorway. Wanda came to the table with the beers and a battered first aid box. Big Joe raised the bottle to his mouth and inhaled half of it. He put it down and belched.

Wanda smiled. "Always did like to see men enjoyin' their time."

She knelt down in front of Elbow to have a closer look at his knee. Arnie looked up from his newspaper behind the bar to keep an eye on the table with the two beers.

"You got a bad cut there, Elbow." Wanda ran a red, painted fingernail up the side of his leg. "I might have to cut off the jeans the rest of the way round to get at it proper like." She smiled.

From where he sat, Elbow could see down a good bit of her cleavage. He took a long swig from his bottle. "Sure, Wanda, anything that helps," he said friendly like. She took a large, shiny, metal scissors out of the first aid box and started cutting his jeans just above the knee. The metal blade felt cool as she slid it between the jeans and his skin. He kept a wary eye on the blade as it neared his inner thigh.

Big Joe took another gulp from his bottle. "You gonna tell me 'bout the boat?" he asked, staring out the door toward the pier.

"Sure, sure. Its kind of funny, really." His mind raced at warp speed trying to think of something funny. "It's like this, see, I was fishing up river from here, just a quiet spot where the current goes kind of still and the fish sometimes rest, and all of a sudden this boat comes by with no one in it. I thought, here's this boat, somebody will miss a thing like that."

Wanda cut through the heavy seam of the jeans with a strong final cut. Elbow flinched. Wanda slipped the cut fabric off of Elbow's leg trailing her fingers against his bare skin. He forced a smile and inspected his upper thighs. Everything vital was still attached.

Wanda ran her bright red nails lightly over the debris clinging to wound. "I better clean this up," she said with a concerned voice. "With a wound like that you don't want to get tomaine or botox or sometin' like that."

Big Joe grunted. Elbow returned to his story. "So I cast my line out toward the boat, hopin' to snag it and reel it in. Got it on the second try. It was heavy and I didn't know if the line would hold but it wasn't in the strong current, you know, and with a little luck it pulled up nice

an' easy next to the tree root I was perched on and just as I almost got my hand on it the line snapped back behind me into the tree and the rod whacked me in the chin right here. See?" He pointed to the bruise on his jaw where one of Louisa's dinner plates clipped him.

Wanda took bright blue gloves out of the box and put them on. "Now this may sling a little." She poured a healthy portion of a bottle of rubbing alcohol over the wound. Elbow let out a string of blue words that scared the resident pelican off the front porch roof. "There, that wasn't so bad was it?" She smiled, picking away at the fish scales, rust and blood in the wound.

Elbow took deep breaths and tried to regain some sort of masculine dignity. His eyes watered and his voice was in the squeaky range. Man, that hurt. He took refuge in his beer bottle with several extra large gulps.

"Maybe you need somethin' stronger, honey. Arnie, pour these two a little whiskey will you?" Wanda told her husband and patted Elbow's other knee with motherly concern. She leaned on his leg as her hands gently worked at cleaning the wound and then ran her hand down his leg to clean off the blood right down to his ankle. Elbow fidgeted in his chair. She smiled at him. Arnie appeared at the table with two whiskeys and gave Elbow a hard look.

"You two want some bar-be-cue?" Wanda asked. "Arnie, get these two some of that brisket from the smoke house. It's real good. Make you forget all about that nasty knee."

After another penetrating look, Arnie ambled off to the smoke house. Wanda resumed her nursing duties. With Arnie busy in the smokehouse, she stroked the wound slowly with a liberal application of anti-bacterial cream. Then she wound a long strip of gauze over the top and made sure to soothingly adjust it behind his knee. "There, that should keep you for a while, honey. You probably should get stitches and one of them DDT shots." She smiled at him again and pulled off

the blue gloves just like she saw them do on TV. Elbow watched as she walked back to the bar, her hips swaying a little from side to side.

"How'd you end up in my boat?" Big Joe said.

Oh yeah, the boat. Elbow drank his shot of whiskey in one gulp and let it burn its way down his throat.

As soon as the whiskey settled into his stomach, Elbow launched back into his story. "Well, when that rod snapped back into that tree and hit me, it kind of caught me off guard. I straight away came off that tree root and fell in the boat. The boat swung off into the current and zip, there I was headin' down stream, my rod and line all tangled up in that tree." He stopped and took a last swig of beer to give Big Joe a chance to digest his tale of woe.

Wanda swiveled over from the bar with a couple of plates of brisket. "Here you are, all hot and smoky from the back. I gave you two extra sauce," Wanda chirped. She walked around the table laying down plastic forks and paper towels for napkins. "How's that knee doin', Elbow? Feelin' a little better?" She gave it a little pat with her hand.

"Yeah, thanks, Wanda. Do you think we could have a couple more beers?"

"Sure thing, sugar."

After he watched Wanda's hips return to the bar, Elbow sat back and studied his luncheon companion. Big Joe didn't bother with the fork. He picked up chunks of brisket with his fingers. He had no use for the paper towel either. He licked his fingers and wiped the remainder on his tee shirt. It was an ample tee shirt, probably size XXXL but it still didn't cover the expanse of his belly. The logo on it was almost obscured with stains from previous briskets and who knew what else. Did it ever get washed? Elbow wondered if he ever took it off or if he just wore shirts until they disintegrated. He probably wore it to bed too. How did a woman like Louisa live with a hefty slob of a man like that?

Wanda brought the beers then made a tour of the other patrons who had wandered in. Big Joe reached for the beer and Elbow caught a glimpse of the hand gun still tucked in Big Joe's belt under his ample roll of stomach.

"Good brisket, huh?" Elbow said.

Big Joe burped again and wiped sauce from his beard off on his sleeve. He leaned back in his chair and looked out the door to the pier. "How'd it get all beat up like that?" he asked.

Big Joe certainly was single minded. When he got on a subject like the boat, he stayed with it like a bull terrier. The bullet holes, Elbow thought. How was he going to explain the bullet holes? Denial was always a good way to go. "It was like that when I saw it, Big Joe, just like someone used it for target practice, only without so much water in the bottom. I had no damn choice but to stay with it until I could get to shore even if it was fillin' up with water. You can see that. Any sane man would have stayed with it rather than risk bein' a gator meal.

"It had a pretty good motor," Big Joe observed.

Elbow thought about the rusty lump of metal clamped to the back of the boat. "Mighty fine. They don't make 'um like that any more."

"Why didn' you use oars?"

"They weren't in the boat! They probably floated down river and are half way to Cuba by now. I had to use my arms to sort of swim and steer the boat anywhere and that wasn't easy with it fillin' up with water like that." At least that part had a ring of truth to it. He rubbed his sore arms to emphasize the point.

Big Joe emptied his beer and pursed his lips together. He was thinking. Elbow started picking fish scales off the front of his shirt in a casual kind of way. His clothes were almost dry and he was trying to think of a way to exit without incurring bullet holes like the boat. "Well, I'm sorry about the boat, Big Joe. You got insurance? You could put in for a new boat. Vandals shot it up and pushed it in the river. You got the evidence right out there under the pier. You did tie it up didn't you?"

Big Joe's eyes got wide. He stood up, almost knocking over the table, and made a rush for the door. The walkway shook as he

thundered down to the pier. The boat was gone. Big Joe knelt down on the pier and pounded it with his fists.

Arnie looked up from his paper. "What's that fool doing beatin' on the pier like that!" He reached for the shotgun he kept behind the bar, then ambled down to the pier.

Elbow thought this was as good a time as any to part company. He sauntered up to the bar and handed Wanda a twenty. "This cover it?" he asked.

"Sure sweetie, you even get change."

"Keep it," he said and gave her a wink.

"Why, thanks!" She filed it away in her cleavage then flashed him bedroom eyes under inch long, fake lashes.

He smiled in return. The Wanda show was always worth it.

Elbow took another glance at the situation on the pier. Arnie was momentarily busy trying to calm Big Joe down so he leaned over the bar and gave Wanda a kiss on the cheek.

"Why, Elbow, you make me blush!" she said.

He knew she probably hadn't blushed since 6th grade, but he played along with the schoolgirl thing. "You should blush more often. Makes your face glow. You did a fine job fixin' up my knee, mighty brave with all that blood."

"Silly, I seen much worse. You know what it's like here on a Saturday night. Everybody gets a little hot and bothered and all that broken glass."

"You're just like an 'Angel of Mercy.'"

"An 'Angel of Mercy,'" she gushed. "Elbow, you are such a tease."

Elbow glanced out at the pier again. The assault on the pier was over and Arnie was heading back with Big Joe.

"Sorry, Wanda, I got to head out," he said.

"You be sure to have someone look after that knee now."

"I'll go to the 'doc-in-the-box' this afternoon."

"Bye, hon. Come back anytime. *Anytime.*"

Elbow gave her another of his boyish grins and headed for the door to the parking lot. He would certainly be back, hopefully when Arnie wasn't there. He thought about what Big Joe would say to Louisa when he got home. Louisa would never tell Big Joe she had a 'visitor'. That would set Big Joe off something fierce. She might make up some story about how someone who looked just like Elbow came into the yard and made off with the boat and how she fired off the shotgun at him but missed. Yeah she was just crazy enough to do that. Better steer clear of both of them for a good while.

Elbow looked around Arnie's parking lot, hoping for some transportation. The motorbike was hidden in a duck blind about a quarter mile from Louisa's. It was a bit of a hike from Arnie's, maybe five miles. Everyone was heading inside for the brisket and liquid refreshment. No one was leaving yet. Nothing for it but to walk.

He started off at a steady pace. He felt like an idiot with mismatched legs on his jeans, one long and the other cut off. His bandaged knee was not happy. The gauze chaffed so he stopped and took it off. The wound started bleeding again so he wrapped the gauze around the knee any way he could. It stung. He limped. The noon sun beat down on his head. Although the cold beer tasted great going down, now it made him hot. He almost yearned for the cool of the river.

The road was a dusty, raised gravel mound cut straight through low, swampy land with an impossible tangle of scrub brush on either side. Every once in a while there were metal culverts underneath to let water flow toward the river. Behind him, in the distance, Elbow could see a cloud of dust from a car or truck coming his way. Please don't let it be Big Joe, he prayed. The truck slowed and stopped. It was Ned Pedit in his poultry truck.

"Hey there, Elbow, what you doin' out here?"

"Just hikiin' up to get my bike."

"Well, hop on back and I'll give you a lift. Sorry I can't let you ride up front but Mono here likes his window seat." Mono was a great dane with a slobber problem. "Give a shout when you want me to stop."

Elbow gave the back of the poultry truck a doubtful glance where cages of unhappy chickens were piled on top of one another and strapped on, but anything was better than sharing the front seat with Mono. Elbow found an empty spot near the tailgate, hoisted himself up and wedged himself in. The truck started with a jerk. The chickens

complained with an angry chorus. The truck slowly got up to speed and a whirlwind of dust and chicken feathers descended from all directions. Elbow pulled his shirt up to cover his nose and mouth.

Four miles of dust and feathers later, Elbow banged on the side and the truck stopped. He un-wedged himself from the space between the wire cages and lowered himself to the ground. The dust cloud following the truck caught up to it. He waved to Ned through the curtain of dust and Ned started up again, putting the ancient truck through a grinding set of gears and a belch of oily exhaust from the tailpipe.

Elbow coughed up a load of chicken feathers and dust and spat it out on the road. Maybe riding up front in Mono's slobber seat wouldn't have been so bad after all. Except for the ode d' dog, the air might have smelled a might fresher than chicken crap. He ran his fingers through his hair to dislodge some feathers and gave his shirt a shake too. From the amount of feathers that fell out he surmised the chickens would be bald by the time they got wherever they were going. He itched. He looked back down the road and saw another cloud of dust coming his way. Time to head for the duck blind and be out of sight in case it was Big Joe.

The blind was on a short stretch of gravel that led back into the swampy brush. It was a lazy structure, built on stilts out of wood scraps and canvas. It overlooked an open stretch of backwater near the river that attracted all kinds of birds that were just dumb enough to think it was safe to stop there.

He lifted the loose drape of canvas on the side of the blind. It was hot and dark inside. The motorbike was just as he left it. He grabbed the handlebars and kicked back the stand to walk it outside. He froze. Something moved. In the dim light he could see eyes and there was a tongue flicking in and out. Oh damn, it was a snake. A big snake. A boa, ten feet at least, wrapped around the the seat and gas tank. Elbow started taking in air and had to remind himself to breathe out. Man, he

hated snakes. He slowly unclenched his hands from the handlebars and backed out of the blind. If that thing wanted the bike, it could have it.

The snake, roused from its nap, tasted the air with its tongue. The intriguing aroma of chicken, fish and brisket caught its attention. It slowly uncoiled from the bike seat, slid over the handlebars and off the front bumper onto the ground to follow the delicious scent out underneath the canvas.

Elbow bent over to try and catch his breath. Nothing like meeting a giant snake, eye to eye in the dark, to suck all the oxygen out of the air. His breathing under control, he straightened up and glanced back at the duck blind. The thing was oozing its way under the canvas, flicking its evil tongue in his direction. The head was as big as a boot! Were boas poisonous? It wasn't a great time to stop and google *boa constrictor*.

The snake slid out into daylight. Its eyes were temporarily blinded but its tongue kept it right on track toward fish guts and barbecue. Elbow was still doing deep breathing exercises, trying to keep from passing out. The snake made steady progress toward its quarry. Elbow backed up and almost stumbled. Think, man, think! He picked up a dead branch. It was a feeble defense. The snake probably knew how to use it. God, it was a monster! Twelve feet at least. It kept coming.

Elbow could hear the car or truck on the road coming closer. If he could time it just right ... Yeah, that was the plan. The truck barreled toward them, oblivious to the drama that was about to unfold.

It was now or never. Elbow sprinted toward the road at full speed. The snake followed. At the last second he dived in front of the truck toward the other side of the road. There was a massive thump. The truck swerved as the driver pushed at unbalanced brakes. The truck ended up sideways on the road about a hundred feet away. Elbow ended up hugging a mangrove bush in the ditch. The snake ended up dead.

The driver exited the truck using every swearword only truckers know as the cloud of road dust enveloped them all. Elbow loosened his

grip on the mangrove branch and untangled his legs. He would count the wounds later.

"What the hell do you think you're doin', runnin' out on the middle of the road like that, you fool?!"

Elbow climbed up the side of the ditch and pointed to the snake. It was stretched out across the road, its tail still twitching.

"Holy Mother of ...! Is that a snake?" the driver asked.

"You saved my life, man," Elbow told him.

The two men inspected the snake. The shear size of the snake removed all the driver's anger. "How long is that thing?"

"I figure twelve feet at least," Elbow remarked. "It'd make a great belt, you know, somethin' to show the ladies."

"I bring that thing home and my wife would run *me* over. Besides, it's got tire tracks on it. Who wants a belt with tire tracks on it.?"

"There's still a couple of feet without tracks on it."

"You keep it. I hate snakes."

"Yeah, me too. It's a guy thing. Adam and Eve and snakes and all that."

"Yeah." The driver looked at his truck. "Hell, how am I gonna get my truck turned around with it sideways like that?"

"Maybe I could help. Six inches or a foot at a time, you could make it. I'll just yell 'stop' so you don't slip in the ditch."

"OK, but yell nice and loud so's I can stay on nice, dry land."

"Right."

It didn't help that the truck had a broken side mirror but after six or seven back and forth tries, the truck was on the road headed in the right direction. The driver shook Elbow's hand before he headed off. Nothing like a giant snake and maneuvering a truck to make best buddies of two guys.

Elbow stood alone in the middle of the road and surveyed the snake. He could maybe do something with it, maybe even sell it. He kicked at the head. Even though two places in the middle of the snake were completely flat, you never knew with a thing as big as that. He picked up the tail and dragged the beast to the side of the road. The snake was heavy, probably weighed more than he did.

He went to retrieve the motorbike. He approached the duck blind with caution. What if the were more of them? Did they mate for life and the other one was waiting for him, ready to coil up and get him?

He slowly lifted the canvas opening on the duck blind. The inside was dark. No yellow eyes looked back at him. So far so good. He inspected the bike. Everything was there that should be there and nothing was there that shouldn't be. He gingerly sat on the seat and walked it out of the blind. Nothing hissed or slithered.

He stopped at the road and pondered what to do with all that snake. It would never fit in the small basket on the back of the bike but it was too tempting to leave for anyone else. He picked up the tail with his fingers and started piling it into the basket. The basket filled rapidly so he draped the rest artistically over the back fender and threaded it gingerly under the seat and around the handlebars. The head ended up almost in his lap which was very unnerving. He secured it all as best he could with his belt.

It was starting to ooze green liquids. It would be a job keeping steady on the bike with all the extra weight. A quick check down the road for approaching dust clouds of cars or trucks and he was off. A quarter mile farther on was Louisa's place. He revved up to full speed, hoping she wasn't out mowing the grass or doing more target practice. He slipped by with no problem.

Why weren't women more flexible, you know, like guys. Why couldn't they just enjoy life as it came? Why did they always want

commitment or jewelry or a poodle or something? Why not just shake hands when things went sour? Why bring out the shotguns?

Elbow reached the junction with the main highway. The ride would be smoother. He turned and eased into traffic. The constrictor's head suddenly shifted position. The green ooze slowly made its way down Elbow's leg and into his shoe. He shivered.

The bike swerved. A neighboring car let loose with a horn serenade and accompanying hand gestures, then passed the bike with a bravado of engine noise. Elbow saluted back with a minimum of fingers.

The landscape abruptly turned from jungle swamp to civilized suburbia. Traffic was a little heavier now in both directions. Elbow concentrated on his driving. He knew the snake was dead, but it seemed to have revived. He watched as the snake's head sank lower and lower down his leg, dragging the rest of its limp body with it until the bike was so heavily loaded on one side that he had to lean precariously to the other side to keep the bike upright. It was no time to be practicing circus moves on a bike with a snake. He slowed down to twenty miles per hour as he made the turn into an intersection.

The snake, lubricated with its own internal ooze, slipped off the bike onto the pavement in the middle of the street. The tail caught in a sprocket on the rear wheel and wound around it until the bulk of the body stopped the bike cold. The bike followed the rules of physics and landed sideways. Elbow hung on for dear life on the up side of the bike as car brakes screeched and metal fenders crunched around him.

He lay there in the middle of the intersection trying to do a mental inventory of parts of his body that had hit the pavement. He was still conscious. That was either a good thing or a bad thing. It would take a minute or two before everything checked in and he knew the full extent of the damage.

His right shoulder seemed to be underneath him and was beginning to sting. He rolled over and used his other hand to explore. He encountered a shredded shirt and what he assumed was blood.

Damn, that was his good shirt. He could have washed all the fish goo and gasoline out of it. Now he would have to go back to the Salvation Army store to find another one.

Sirens sounded in the distance. He propped himself up to take a look around. Three cars, one with a leaking radiator, were sort of tangled together. Chunks of bumpers, headlights, side mirrors and broken glass littered the street.

Sirens sounded closer. Elbow struggled to get up on one knee. His right arm dangled uncooperatively at his side. He took his right hand and shoved it in the front of his shirt like Napoleon and made a monumental effort to stand. Glass crunched under his shoes.

People were beginning to venture out into the street to take pictures of the mangled bumpers and passengers emerging blurry-eyed from their cars. The snake in particular would definitely make the evening news on half a dozen cell phone videos. Two squad cars pulled up into the intersection. Elbow remembered he didn't exactly have a pleasant working relationship with the local constabulary. Definitely time to go. His head whirled. He was a little wobbly as he made his way over to the sidewalk. A kind bystander caught him before he hit the ground.

"Many thanks," Elbow told him. "Man, did you see the size of that snake? It just up and tangled in that bike. Must have come out of that ditch over there." Good plan. Blame it on the snake. It was the damn snake's fault anyway. The guy holding him up would probably blab the snake story to anyone who asked.

An ambulance arrived. Elbow faded into the back of the gaping crowd and limped away, leaning up against the chainlink fence every once in a while. Time to put as much distance as he could between himself and the cops on the corner. It would take them a long while to sort it all out. If he was lucky they wouldn't check on the bike for several days. It wasn't really his bike anyway. He had sort of "borrowed" it from a friend. Well, the woman wasn't exactly a friend anymore but

she might be glad to know what happened to the bike. All the same, she might definitely be unhappy about its present condition with snake guts wrapped around the rear wheel. Better lay low for a while.

Elbow ducked into an alley the first chance he got. Out of sight, out of mind. The fewer people saw him with his mismatched jean legs and shredded, bloody shirt the better it would be. It was a long trek to the place he shared with two other room mates in an abandoned warehouse, along a weed choked canal. They had it decked out pretty nice. Running water and everything.

Things were beginning to ache and sting. He concentrated on putting one foot in front of the other, resting on garbage cans every once in a while as he made his way through deserted alleyways. All he could think about was getting back to the warehouse and his nice bed. He had made it himself out of salvaged styrofoam and foam pads from the exercise center dumpster.

He turned the last corner and looked behind him. No one in sight. He looked at the pavement too. No blood drops. It was safe to go in. If anyone even cared to look, they would need bloodhounds to find him.

He approached the large metal door next to the former loading dock. A torn electrical cord dangled from above. He pulled on it. A chorus of metallic noise sounded inside. A moment later a window cranked open above him.

"Elbow, what you doing out there? Forget your key?" the man laughed.

"Just let me in, doofus! Can't you see I'm hurtin' here?"

"Be right down."

A few moments later the metal door protested as it was forced to move on rusty hinges. A tall, skinny man with a reddish beard and paint splattered clothes propped it open with a chunk of concrete.

"Man, you look worse than usual. Who beat you up like that? You owe somebody money or something?"

"Just help me get to my bed. I got to lay down and rest up."

"Yeah. Sure, sure. Just let me close the door." He kicked the concrete chunk out of the way and the door groaned its way back into place and banged shut.

Elbow leaned on a metal pillar for support. Things were really beginning to hurt. "Red, you got any more of those white pills?"

"You mean the painkiller ones or the constipation ones?"

"Do I look like I'm constipated? I'm standin' here drippin' bodily fluids! My arm doesn't work and half my jeans are torn off!"

"Okay, okay, I'll get you to bed then I'll find them. How'd you get like this anyway?"

"It's a long story but I've been shot at, almost gator lunch in the river, attacked by a giant snake and surrounded by bumper banging cars with a death wish!"

"All in one day? You're puttin' me on."

"No! Now just get me to bed."

Elbow leaned on Red as the two men staggered their way across the empty expanse of warehouse floor toward a plastic draped section in the back corner. Red held the plastic sheet aside to let them pass through into Elbow's inner sanctum. It would never appear in *Better Homes and Gardens*, Elbow's taste was somewhere between industrial shabby-chic and hoarder's anonymous, but it had a bed and there was a fridge that held basic, stimulating beverages. With Red's help, Elbow lowered himself down onto the soft comfort of the styrofoam bed.

"Thanks, Red, now find me some of those pills, will you?"

"Sure, rest easy." Red returned with two white pills from his private stash. "Careful you don't take too many at one time, you know. I only got four."

Elbow popped the two pills in his mouth and washed them down with leftover beer from breakfast. He leaned back and allowed his body to relax. The pain settled into an annoying throb. He looked at the peeling paint on the ceiling and the graceful swag of dusty spider web in the corner. 'Home' he said to himself. He was free and home. His

eyelids grew heavy and the pain-numbing oblivion of sleep overtook him.

Elbow woke up with a start. The room was dark, illuminated only by the orange glow of a safety light in the alley next door. Something or someone was in the room. There it was again, that rustling sound. A light suddenly flashed in his eyes.

"Elbow! You lowlife scumbag! What you do with my Pepito?"

"What?"

"My bird. My cockatoo? Pepito! You always teasing him."

It was Rosita, Red's girlfriend, all five feet, feisty two inches of her, looking for her damn bird, the one that always took special aim at his shirt when it wanted to "unload".

"You got him in here?"

"No, get that light out of my eyes. I'm tryin' to sleep."

"You look like shit and you smell bad too. My bird maybe he don't want to come near you so much."

"That would be just fine with me. I got enough poop on me right now to make even 'dear Pepito' jealous." Elbow reached over with his good arm to turn on the lava lamp and get Rosita's flashlight out of his face.

"What happen to you? You all messed up."

"Yeah, well, it was one hell of a day."

"What happen to your arm? It don't work?"

"I don't think it's broken, just out of the socket. I can't lift it."

"Ok, I fix."

"What do you mean you'll 'fix'."

"I fix. You sit in chair. I pull, I twist, I push. It hurt like hell then it better. Poof, I fix."

"No 'poof you fix'. I'll go to the doc in the box on the corner. He'll patch me up."

"No good. They take him away two days ago. I watch out window. Police with guns. They take him away. Maybe bad drugs, maybe

somebody die. I don't know. You sit in chair. I fix. Then you take shower. You stink."

Elbow considered his options. The doc on the corner never bothered too much with formalities like name and address if wounds were serious enough to attract police attention. A few extra dollars and there were no questions. A hospital would ask questions, maybe even have a list of interesting patients to look out for. It was Rosita or walk around with a right arm hanging like limp spaghetti.

He headed for the fridge. The pills were wearing off. Time to use something reliable like whiskey. After several healthy doses from the bottle, he sat down in the chair. He smiled at Rosita. She was Red's model. She wore crazy combinations of clothes in wild colors but didn't mind taking them all off at the slightest provocation. Now she was all business. She took off her blouse to have complete freedom in her bra. Elbow took another swig of whiskey.

"So Rosita, how do you know how to do this?"

"I do all the time for my uncle. He maybe has not so good time with police sometimes. Handcuffs always behind his back and maybe he fight a little. I seen a doctor do it once. I put it back many times. I know how."

Elbow took a few more swigs from the bottle and hoped for the best.

"You yell loud if you want, but I just do this, Okay?"

"Okay." His world was getting fuzzy.

Rosita grabbed his right hand and arm and slowly rotated everything carefully. With one quick move she shoved as hard as she could.

"YAAAHHHHH!!!" Elbow almost fell off the chair.

"Ok, you good now," Rosita told him.

"What do you mean it's good now! It hurts like hell!"

"Yeah, but it move now." She patted the shoulder. "It maybe puff up here. You got ice in you box? Take a shower. Now you stink worse. You

see Pepito, you tell me, Okay?" She put her shirt back on, took a drink from his whiskey bottle and walked out.

Elbow sat in the chair moving his fingers. His shoulder was sore but it worked like a shoulder again. One more helping of medicinal whiskey and he was ready to face the shower. When he stood up, the room seemed to have other ideas, spinning around at a crazy angle. Elbow made a dive for the bed. He was down for the count.

The steady drip, drip of water on his forehead made Elbow open one eye. There was gray daylight. It was morning. The sound of rolling thunder shook the bed and got his attention. He raised up his head. Why was he half on the bed and half on the floor? He moved his arm and remembered with painful clarity. Oh yeah, the snake, the bike, the whiskey and Rosita.

He made a huge effort to move. There wasn't a single part of his body that didn't complain. Thunder shook everything again. Damn, it was raining. The roof leaked. He got to his feet and reached for some plastic to cover the bed before the foam soaked up water like a sponge. The bottle of whiskey was still there beside the chair. Ah, an offering to appease the headache god attacking the inside of his skull.

He took a deep breath and coughed. The foul smell in the room wasn't from a fresh coating of mold on the wall beneath the leaking windows. It was him. Definitely time for a shower.

The bathroom was his own dubious construction and a bit drafty at times because it was open to the steel rafters in the middle of the warehouse. There was a drain in the floor that emptied into the debris choked canal outside. A couple of wooden shipping pallets to stand on covered the drain. Some plastic sheets were stapled to two by four uprights at each corner. Add a garden hose from the barrels on the roof and presto, instant shower. Not glamorous, but the water was warm most of the time. There was also a stolen Porta Potty parked in the corner, rigged to drain outside too. All the comforts of home.

Elbow carefully removed his clothes. Dried blood from the pavement burn on his arm stuck to the tiny scratches and hurt like a hundred stinging bees as the shirt peeled away. He took another swallow of 'breakfast." His tennis shoes were coated with blood and snake goo so he pried them off and tossed them in a corner. He slid off his jeans over the dirty gauze bandage wrapped around his knee, then

carefully removed the bandage to get a good look at the cut. It looked Okay. Wanda and her bright red fingernails had done a pretty good job.

His reflection in the broken mirror over the industrial sink was a little cruel. The bruise on his chin, where Louisa's plate had clipped him, was a deep purple. There was another bruise above his right eyebrow that was migrating downward around his eye. Damn, where did that one come from? He didn't exactly remember, maybe the bike accident. He inspected the rest of his torso. There was a large blue bruise on his right hip. That one he remembered when he kissed the pavement. All in all it wasn't too bad. He often looked much worse after a bar fight.

He lathered up the day old stubble on his chin and attempted to shave. The ladies liked it smooth. His shoulder was sore. His right hand didn't reach too far. He had to use his left. The result wasn't exactly smooth. Patchy would be a better word. It would do. The ladies wouldn't look much past the black eye anyway.

He stepped into the plastic shower enclosure and turned on the spray head at the end of the hose. A steady stream of lukewarm water poured out, then turned warm as the hose emptied the long connection between the shower and the barrel. He let it play on his head and run down his body. The cuts on his arm screamed a bit but the warmth felt great on the shoulder and hip. He turned the water off and lathered up with Manly Musk shower gel. The cuts on his arm didn't like the gel much either. He rinsed it off and watched as all the blood, fish scales, barbecue sauce, chicken feathers and snake guts slipped through the slats of the shipping pallet, circled the drain and disappeared.

After gingerly drying off with a beach towel, he applied fresh bandaids to the more sensitive spots, then selected a few semi-clean items from the box under his bed and dressed. The shirt and jeans covered up the worst of the injuries, and if he could suck it up he could disguise the limp as a swagger. Anyway, it felt good to be rid of all the crusty dirt.

Next item of business was breakfast. His watch said twelve twenty-five. Okay, so it was lunch. Potato, po-TAH-to. He put a spoonful of instant coffee in the cup next to the bed, added water and nuked it. He poured out imitation Cocoa Puffs into a bowl and gave the milk from the fridge a sniff test. It would pass. He sat at the card table to eat and watched rain drops trickle down the window. Afternoon showers built up during the heat of the day and dumped their load quickly. It seemed to be God's plan to keep the mosquitos happy. When rain started in the morning, it usually lasted all day. Bummer.

SPLAT! A large, white glob dropped on the edge of his coffee cup. Elbow looked up. Somewhere in the dim, upper reaches of the rusty, metal grid ceiling he could see white feathers.

"'Poopito!' You miserable excuse for a bird! You did that on purpose! You just stored it up, didn't you, and waited until I was eating and let go on my coffee cup!"

SPLAT! Another salvo dropped from above, this time hitting the cereal bowl dead center.

"If I ever get my hands on you I'll ... I'll strangle your evil little neck!" Elbow was enraged. The bird had pooped in his shoe, shredded his driver's license, decorated his shoulders and even walked boldly across the table one night to drop a cockroach in his beer. Enough was enough. "This is war, 'Poopito'. You against me! WAR!"

Elbow sat and thought about it. The bird had been on the loose since yesterday. It had plenty of access to water but nothing to eat except maybe cockroaches taking refuge from the rain. It really liked seeds. He didn't have any seeds, but what about Cocoa Puffs? Yeah, spread some of those on the floor, put a cardboard box over them with a stick holding up one side, attach a string and wham! when the 'winged wonder' swooped in for lunch, pull on the string and he's trapped. Perfect. What could go wrong?!

He searched for just the right box. One Amazon box that didn't exactly have <u>his</u> name on the label was the right size. He took the stick that propped open the vent above the plastic shower and unraveled some nylon fishing line from the rod he kept near the bed. That little feathered son-of-a-gun was in for it now.

He assembled the trap in the middle of the warehouse floor so the bird would have a clear view of the Cocoa Puffs from wherever he might be lurking in the rafters. The fishing line was rigged on the stick, the box propped up and Elbow casually meandered back to the table and pretended to read the sports section of yesterday's newspaper. He kept a keen eye on the box and a firm hold on the fishing line. There were flutterings in the girders above him.

"Come on, you little poop master. Come to papa," Elbow muttered under his breath.

There were more flutters. Suddenly the white bird swooped down and landed on top of the box. Elbow tried to remain calm. "Not on *top* on the box, you idiot" he hissed.

Pepito cocked his head sideways as if to survey the situation. He blessed the box with a blob of white. Elbow held it in and willed himself to ignore it and be patient. "Come on, come on, those are Cocoa Puffs. You know you want them."

The bird hopped to the concrete floor to look under the box. Elbow's fingers twitched with anticipation.

"Just a little more, just a little more."

The bird tested the waters by picking up one nugget and hopping a few feet away to eat it.

"Yes, yes, yum, yum. Have some more," Elbow told the bird from behind the newspaper.

The bird hopped back to the box and went farther into the shadow underneath for another morsel. Elbow held his breath.

"One hop more. Please, just one more hop."

The bird hopped. Elbow pulled the line. The stick collapsed, the box came down and Elbow almost fell off his chair in a rush to claim his prize. Pepito screeched and thrashed inside the box, moving it sideways across the floor. Elbow put his foot on the top to hold it still.

"You're mine now, you little poop artist! Mine! All mine!"

But a bird in the box isn't always worth one in the hand. Elbow reached under the side of the box to grab it. Pepito was having none of it. He screeched. Feathers flew in all directions. Just as Elbow gripped one of the bird's legs, the bird clamped down on his finger with its vice-like beak and refused to let go.

"Yeeeooowww!" Elbow yelled, waving his hand in the air with the bird still attached. Blood dripped from his finger. He grabbed the bird's body and stuffed it under his arm. The bird let go of the finger in order to get a grip in Elbow's armpit.

"Oh no you don't, you nasty, foul, feathered, freaking ..."

He grabbed the bird from the back and held its wings closed. He kicked the empty Amazon box open and shoved the bird back inside. Next he pushed the flaps in place, grabbed the nylon fishing line and sealed it closed. He stepped back. Man, his finger hurt! That damn bird was a menace to society.

Elbow ran some water from the shower hose over the bleeding finger. The bird had bitten it deep. He reached for the box of Bandaids and pressed one around the cut as tightly as he could. He followed that with a large wad of toilet paper and a bit of masking tape just in case it kept bleeding.

He walked back to the box. It was quiet. No screeching, no fluttering. Was it dead? He wasn't that rough with it, but you never knew. He walked around the box several times and sat down to think about what to do next. It was Rosita's little darling bird. She might not be too happy to hear about its demise. The woman had a bit of a temper. He might find her aiming more than a flashlight in his face some night if she thought he had anything to do with ending Pepito's avian career.

Then he heard it. A crunching sound. It was coming from inside the box. The cheeky bird was eating Cocoa Puffs inside the box! The crunching noise stopped. There was a tearing noise. The bird was ripping pieces of cardboard off the inside of the box with his beak. Time to do something before it shredded an escape hatch. Elbow lifted the box gingerly off the floor. The box went quiet.

"Ok, you crazy cockatoo, I'll take you up to 'mama Rosita', but if you spill even one word about this adventure, I will have <u>you</u> for breakfast instead of Cocoa Puffs. You got that straight?" The bird stripped off another chunk of cardboard.

Elbow climbed the metal stairs to the second floor. The small, upper floor used to be office space, now it was Red's domain, his and Rosita's. Red was a painter. Rosita was his model. She came one day and just stayed. She said she was from Puerto Rico but Elbow had his doubts. She had a gun and he had no trouble believing she knew how to use it.

He knocked on the door and entered Red's studio. Rosita was posed stark nude on a wicker lounge chair. Her dark hair was spread out against jade green cushions that made her skin look milky white. Her figure was perhaps a trifle too plump around the middle and thighs to be perfect, but Red liked her. The room was lined with paintings of her, all nude. Nude was Rosita's natural state. She wore clothes or didn't as it suited her. Elbow stood in the doorway and admired the pose. Red stopped painting and wiped his brush on his pants

"Elbow, come in, come in. I was just starting a new painting. How you feeling? Rosita said she fixed your arm."

"Yeah, it's stiff but it works. Thanks, Rosita. I brought you a little present." He held up the box.

"A present? For me?" Rosita said as she slid off the cushions and draped a fringed shawl sideways across her body to tie it at the shoulder. It didn't cover everything, but it was a polite gesture.

The bird started scuffling inside the box at the sound of her voice. Elbow undid the fishing line and carefully lifted the first cardboard flap. Pepito burst out of the box in a mad scramble of white feathers and squawking noise. He landed on a lampshade and continued a barrage of complaints against the indignities of the box, Elbow and even the Cocoa Puffs.

"You found him! My sweet little Pepito! You bad little baby," she cooed as she lifted him off the lampshade and offered soothing kisses. The bird offered kisses back with his beak.

"He all messed up. He got feathers missing. What you do to him?" She stroked its head.

"Nothing, Rosita. He was up in the rafters. It's pretty rough up there. I don't know, maybe he's molting. I put some Cocoa Puffs on the floor and he was pretty hungry, so when he flew down I just put the box on top of him."

"You feed him Cocoa Puffs?! They no good for him. He like papaya, sometimes mango. No Cocoa Puffs!"

"I didn't have any papaya. He's back now. He seems pretty upset. You better keep him in the cage for a while. Give him some water, maybe a valium. If he gets loose again who knows what might get him. There are rats or bats up in the rafters."

"Oh my little Pepito! You were so brave. Mommy going to give you some nuts. You like nuts. I take care of my little Pepito."

Elbow and Red looked at the mini love fest going on between the bird and Rosita. They rolled their eyes heavenward and exchanged a look between them.

"Maybe he was just bored, you know, maybe he needs a mate," Red suggested.

Elbow blanched at the thought of two idiot cockatoos dive bombing him from the rafters and possibly even little baby Pepitos. One was too many already.

"I take care of him. He sleep with me tonight. I take care of my little Pepito."

"Now look here, Rosita, I can't sleep with that bird perched on the headboard over my pillow," Red complained. "He lets out one of those screeches at two in the morning and I think the the cops are raiding the place."

"He sleep with me! You don't like it you sleep on the lounge chair! Pepito needs his mommy Rosita."

Red threw his paint brush on the floor. Elbow recognized the signs. A large fight was brewing. Time to make an exit. He backed out of the

room and tip-toed down the stairs. Somebody was definitely sleeping on the wicker lounge chair tonight and he guessed it wasn't the bird.

The fight went on for almost an hour. There were loud outbursts from all parties, including Pepito, and something got smashed on the floor, but no gunshots. If it followed the pattern of their other fights, it would end up a standoff followed by a passionate twenty-four hour 'apology'.

Elbow removed the cereal bowl from the table and rinsed it out in the shower before the small parade of ants began to take an interest in it. Once ants got the idea there was something edible hanging around, they were stubborn about giving it up, even if it wasn't there anymore. A couple of cockroaches were exploring the Cocoa Puff's on the floor. He let them duke it out. Winner take all.

He took a beer from the fridge and sat at the card table to watch some news on the jerry-rigged computer screen. The weather map showed a hopeful clearing of rain clouds by early evening. The racetrack would be faster tomorrow. Maybe he could pick a few winners.

Then suddenly, there it was on the late afternoon news, video of the snake, his snake, in the middle of the intersection. Some newswoman was yammering on about the possibility of an invasion of giant snakes in Miami and what were the local authorities going to do about it. Elbow laughed. He watched the rest of the newscast with interest to see if anyone caught him slinking away from the scene of the crime. The focus was definitely on the snake with its tail wound around the rear wheel of the motorbike. Damn, he sure was going to miss that bike.

Suddenly it was all quiet upstairs. Red and Rosita were either recovering from their wounds or patching things up in bed and the bird was wallowing in nuts and papaya. Elbow grimaced. Papaya. No wonder the little pooper let loose everywhere. Right now he was probably loading up big time for the next assault.

He looked at his face in the mirror. Not too bad. Even his arm was feeling better. At least he could use it to lift a libation to his mouth. Time to visit the Flaming Flamingo Bar and Grill to see what the rest of the world was doing. He splashed on some after shave, checked his tee shirt for any white streaks and headed out the door. The rain had stopped, but the air was heavy with humidity. Crickets and cicadas whistled urgent mating calls in the darkness.

Elbow slipped his right thumb in one of his jean belt loops as sort of a substitute sling. He practiced his limp/swagger walk as he avoided the puddles in the deserted truck yard, then moved along the wall of the building next door and around the corner into the glare of the street. Several establishments advertised in bright, blaring neon. At the end of the block, the Flaming Flamingo sign featured a pink dancing bird with shapely legs above the door. There were the usual number of customers standing outside, filling their lungs with nicotine and other addicting substances. He grabbed the door handle and pulled the door open. The inside was a dark cave compared to the neon extravaganza outside. The main illumination came from the glass shelves displaying bottles of booze behind the bar.

He waved a high sign to Eddy, the bouncer at the door, and made his way to the bar. It was dark enough that Elbow reasoned no one would notice his black eye if he faced away from the light. He ordered a beer and a burger and casually glanced around to survey the crowd. There were several promising ladies of his acquaintance and several he might want to avoid. Not wanting to start any uncomfortable

conversations he gave the bartender a nod that he was headed to the back room. There were booths back there, a couple of pool tables and a bit more room to move around. He took a seat on one of the tall stools near the pool tables to watch one of the locals make mincemeat out of a young hotshot who looked like he was straight out of high school. The kid was an easy mark and didn't have a chance.

The waitress found him to deliver the burger and the beer. Elbow paid her and included a generous tip. She was a sweet looker and he might want her to remember him later. He downed a few swallows of beer and dove into the burger. The Flamingo's burgers weren't the best but after nothing but whiskey and Cocoa Puffs, it was a treat. It was juicy and generous. He felt like a king.

"Well, well, well, if it isn't the wandering Elbow. You're lookin' a little rough there, sugar."

Elbow looked up. Oh hell, it was Brenda. He washed the last of the burger down with the last of the beer. "How you doing, Brenda? You're looking mighty fine tonight."

"Why, thank you." She moved closer and sat on the stool next to him.

Elbow admired her curves and the way she packaged them in a bright green, knit dress. She crossed her legs, revealing a bit more thigh. Elbow admired that too, but he was wary. Brenda was one of those women who looked all tasty but could spit venom.

"How'd you get that eye? You been mixin' it up with Red and Rosita?"

Elbow twitched a little. His mind raced to come up with a good story, one that wouldn't involve the motorbike he had "borrowed" from Brenda's front porch. "Nothing like that. It was at Arnie's pier. I was helping Big Joe with his boat when this big gator come up behind and bashed at it with his tail and I fell into one of those posts. Skinned my knee too. Big Joe pumped a couple shots into the water after it but it got away. They fixed me up real good." At least part of it was true and

he wouldn't have to think too hard to remember it if he was quizzed in the future.

Brenda flashed him one of her twenty-carat zircon smiles. "You're putin' me on. A gator? You sure it wasn't one of those giant snakes?"

Elbow sensed she had a hint that maybe his story was bogus. "You saw that on TV too? Man, a snake as big as that crawling up on the street. Gives me the creeps."

Brenda wiped the smile off her face. "Yeah, me too! And I got a good look at the motorbike that snake was tangled up in. The police even came to my door. They said it was mine. I told them some lowlife idiot stole it from my porch."

"Imagine that. Your bike shows up on TV with an attack of the giant snakes. The reporter said there was going to be an investigation of giant snakes invading Miami."

"Giant snakes, my Aunt Fanny! That snake was wrapped around that bike by another snake!"

"Whoa, Brenda, you're gettin' all up and bothered like I had something to do with it. I was at Arnie's yesterday. I didn't have a bike. You just ask them, they'll tell you."

"How did you get out there, fly?"

"I bummed a ride, like usual."

"With who?"

"Ned Pedit, you know, Pedit's Perfect Poultry, he'll tell you. He was taking a load of chickens somewhere. Man, they were noisy."

Her eyes narrowed to slits under her inch long, fake lashes. She was almost buying it.

Elbow flashed her one of his winning grins. "Can I buy you something? A beer maybe?"

"Yeah, why not. Make sure it's cold. It's all hot and sticky in here tonight. I got to go powder my nose." She walked off toward the "Gents and Dames" sign in the back. Elbow observed her green dress attracted a lot attention as it swayed its way between the chairs and tables.

He breathed a little easier. Brenda could be pretty intense if she wanted. Her cousin Eddy, the bouncer, was not shy about roughing people up if she told him to. Still, she was <u>very</u> fine company when she had a few drinks and you got her in a good mood. Elbow had nothing better to do. She might be worth a try. He caught the waitress' eye and ordered two beers.

Brenda returned from the "Dames" with a fresh coat of pink lipstick on her lips. A nice look with her reddish hair and green dress. Elbow appreciated the effort. She was sprucing up a bit. It was a good sign. She sat next to him on the high stools and crossed her legs.

"So Elbow, I haven't seen you here in a while. What have you been doing besides wrestling alligators?"

"Not a lot. A few odd jobs here and there, you know, for beer money. I'm always looking. You know anyone who might need something done?"

"Yeah, how are you at scraping snake off a motorbike? The police said I can have it back tomorrow but they weren't going to remove the snake from the back wheel."

"Sure, I could give it a shot. Even fix the wheel if it was messed up." He gave her another smile to cement the deal.

The beers arrived. He gave the waitress a smile and motioned to keep the beers coming. If he remembered right, Brenda got pretty friendly after five or six and she was primed with a few already. To him, beer was like pop. He might feel it in the morning but he could keep up with her all night, no problem. Music started on the juke box.

"Hey, let's dance. It's nice and slow." Brenda stood up and grabbed his hand to lead him out to the small dance floor.

Elbow made a pretense of adjusting the lower legs on his jeans to give his hip a chance to get used to standing. Out on the dance floor, he put her arms around his neck and circled her waist with his arms. It was pretty cozy and he didn't have to move his sore shoulder any more

than necessary. The slow dance suited his hip fine too. All he had to do was sort of stand in one place and shuffle. Piece of cake.

Brenda wanted to get extra cozy. Elbow figured it must be his Manly Musk after shave. He didn't object. She nuzzled her head next to his. If he played his cards right it might be a cozy night too. You never knew with Brenda. If she got on the snake idea again it could go south real quick. Play it cool, he told himself. Let her make the moves.

The night thumped on as the jukebox got lots of action. At closing time Elbow was lip-locked with Brenda in a back booth. She was certainly frisky. She stumbled a little as they exited the Flaming Flamingo around two a.m. Elbow held her up with his good arm. Off they went down the street, weaving a bit on the sidewalk. Brenda wanted to sing. He kept her upright until they got to her cinderblock bungalow several blocks away. She leaned against the door while Elbow used her key to open it. She wanted another kiss and they almost tumbled into the living room together.

He managed to steer her toward the bedroom where she began removing her clothes as if they were on fire. She had a tattoo on her right shoulder. Elbow generally liked tattoos on women but this one said "Pete" inside a red heart. Who the hell was Pete and did he live in her house? There was nothing worse than running into an annoyed boyfriend when you are in bed with a woman wearing his heart tattooed on her shoulder. Awkward, maybe even fatal. Brenda started pulling at his tee shirt. She was a bit blitzed. He would have to keep it friendly.

"Whoa, Brenda, that's some tattoo you're wearing. Who's this Pete fellow?"

"You don't like my tattoo?"

"It's great. Who's Pete?"

"My rotten ex, my dirty, rotten, stinkin' ex!"

"He doesn't live here does he?"

"Not any more. I tossed him out! Threw all his stuff on the front lawn." She started laughing. In an instant it turned to tears.

Elbow rolled his eyes toward heaven. This would either turn into a sob fest or, if he was lucky and played the sympathy card right, it could be one of the best nights of his life. He cradled her in his arms.

"You deserve better. You are one of the hottest ladies on the street. Why, I couldn't take my eyes off of you when I saw you tonight."

"Really?"

"Oh yeah. Super hot."

She reached under his tee shirt to pull it off over his head. He winced as it tugged on his right arm, but hell, she was primed with tears and everything.

Bingo! Jackpot!

"Yip!"

Elbow rolled over, blinked his eyes and shut them again. Sunlight was pouring in through a window. This wasn't his room. There were sheets on the bed. Where the hell was he?

"Yip, Yip."

Elbow's ears recoiled. Was that a dog?

"Yip!"

He felt a wet tongue lick the side of his face. It had a distinctive doggy odor.

"Yip!"

Where was the little yipper? He opened his eyes. Gypsy wagged her little tail and licked his nose. Elbow pushed the happy, hairy face away from him. What time was it? He sat up. Gypsy wagged her tail non-stop and did circles on the bed.

"Yip!"

"Enough with the yipping already! Can't a guy have a hangover in peace?" He sat on the edge of the bed. Slowly, the night before came into focus. Brenda. He was at Brenda's. Her bedroom. Her dog.

Gypsy dropped a pink ball in his lap. Elbow picked it up and threw it into the hallway where he heard it bounce off several walls and hit something metallic. The dog sailed off the bed into the hallway in a frenzy of excitement.

"Yip, yip, yip!"

Elbow kicked the door closed with his foot. He laid back on the bed. It had been one of those nights a guy dreams about. Brenda was certainly hot to trot and she was so insistent. It didn't seem to matter that his shoulder cramped up or his hip looked like raw meat. The perfect ending to an interesting day and it only cost him ten beers. Now if he could just find his clothes. Brenda was a little exuberant removing them last night. They could be anywhere.

Gypsy gave a muffled Yip! behind the door.

Damn, the shih tziu found the ball. Now she'll be a real pest. What was it with dogs and balls? They'll chase them till they drop. He laughed. Pythons don't chase balls, they chase shih tzius. Where was a snake when you needed one?

He found his t-shirt draped over the chair on the other side of the room. His jeans were where he dropped them, tangled in the blanket on the floor. One of his tennis shoes was playing hide and seek. He found it on top of the bookcase. It had been a wild night.

Brenda opened the bedroom door. She wasn't looking quite as fine as the night before. Her hair was uncombed and she was pale without the pink lipstick. There were dark circles under her eyes. She was hugging a cup of coffee. Hangovers were a bummer.

"Morning." He gave her a sympathetic smile.

"Hmmm," she grunted. Gypsy followed her into the room, toenails clicking on the tile floor.

"Yip!"

"Hush, Gypsy, Mommy has a headache." She reached down to the floor to pick up the fluff ball and almost fell over.

Elbow caught her just in time. "Whoa, Brenda, easy, honey."

"Don't you honey me!"

Elbow went on alert. Brenda was slipping into venom mode. Pretty soon everything from her headache to global warming would be his fault. Time to exit. He led her gently to the bed and eased her down onto a pillow. He took the coffee cup and dog out of her hands, closed the curtains and backed out of the room. Gypsy licked his face.

"Enough licking! I'll find you something to eat, and then I'm off before Mommy revives and remembers I bought her the beer that made her head explode." He set Gypsy down on the kitchen floor. She immediately headed for the corner cabinet and sat in front of it, waiting expectantly. "Dog food's in there I guess. Okay, what will it be, kibble or kibble?" He removed the bag and poured a hefty amount in her pink

dish. Gypsy dove into it with gusto. The water bowl was empty so he filled that up too. He turned to leave. Gypsy stopped gulping down food. She ran into the living room to retrieve her ball, then ran to the front door and dropped the ball at his feet.

"Yip!"

"Okay, one more time." With one hand on the door handle, Elbow picked up the ball and threw it against the wall. It careened into the kitchen. Gypsy skittered across the floor in pursuit. There was a crash and the sound of kibble scattering across the tile. Elbow hurried through the front door and closed it behind him. Better leave and let Gypsy worry about it.

Outside the front door he almost tripped. The police had deposited the motorbike right in the middle of the porch. The bulk of the snake had been cut off, leaving only the tail entangled in the wheel. Flies were beginning to take an interest.

Elbow considered the possibilities. He could leave it there for Brenda to find when she finally woke up ... or he could just sort of take it back to the warehouse and work on it there. No need to tell Brenda he had it. He could fix it and use it for a while and then surprise her. Yeah. Great plan.

The back wheel of the motorbike was locked up tight with the snake. The only way to move it was to lift up the back and balance it all on the front tire to wheel it to the warehouse. Damn, the thing was heavy and awkward. Steering it was an upside down, backwards kind of thing. Elbow reasoned he better stick to back alleys rather than risk someone seeing him on the street, then he could slip through the back yard of the Mexican restaurant and along the weedy canal until he was home free.

The day was turning hot and humid. The sun beat down at its tourist postcard best. The bike felt heavier with every step. Oil seeped from the gears onto his tee shirt and down his jeans. The snake was decomposing fast. The smell was getting intense. Every time he passed a garbage can, the swarm of flies increased, buzzing as they fought for room around the rotting end of the snake.

He finally maneuvered the bike through the opening in the fence into the rear yard of the Mexican restaurant. At least there it was safe to put it down and rest for a few minutes. His shoulder was sore. He was tired of limping. The flies were beginning to land on him too. The sooner he got to the warehouse, the sooner he could remove the wheel and dump the python tail in the canal. Then the fly fest would be over.

He got the bike upright again and propped it on his shoulder. The flies didn't take to being disturbed from their giddy, dead python feast. They swarmed up, almost enveloping the bike like some bizarre science fiction nightmare. Elbow fought for breathing room. Swatting did no good. Better hurry.

Man he was tired. The last hundred feet or so followed the narrow path along the edge of the old canal at the side of the warehouse. The bike wanted to go sideways on the path. Only a few more yards to go. No one used the path much. Tall weeds grew out from the side of the building. He wished he had a machete.

He set the bike down to bend back a few stray trees blocking the way. Then he heard it, the sound of metal hitting the broken, concrete edge of the canal and then a splash. He turned around just in time to see the bike disappear over the edge and sink into the muddy depths.

"No! No! No!" he yelled in vain to the gods.

He sat down and looked at the water in stunned silence as bubbles and an oil slick rose to the surface. In a few minutes, part of one wheel poked up into the air. It was still attached to the bike. He tried to grab

it but it was too far out from the edge. Maybe he could reach it with his foot and nudge it closer to the side so he could pull it up with his hands.

Lying down on the concrete edge and extending his leg out over the water, his foot barely touched the tire. His hip complained like crazy but it was either that or lose the bike forever. Slowly, painfully, he managed to hook his foot on one of the spokes of the wheel and pull it a few inches closer. One of the handlebars was just visible in the murky water. He grabbed it and pulled. The rest of the bike was already settling into the foul muck at the bottom of the canal. It was stuck.

How was he going to get it out of there? It wasn't budging, but letting go would allow it to sink all the way in, and he couldn't lie there all day and hold it. He looked around for inspiration. His jeans. Take them off, tie one leg to the handlebar and the other to a small tree or something near the building. Then he could go inside and find a board to pry it loose from the bottom and hoist it up on the path.

Elbow had never been a Boy Scout. His knot tying skills were primitive at best and jeans were not the ideal material to tie up anything. While lying on the ground and one hand still holding onto the bike, he managed to unzip the jeans and remove them from one leg and then the other. So far so good. The hard part was reaching far enough out over the water to do a decent job tying a knot with only one good arm. The other arm, attached to the sore shoulder was useless for lifting or stretching.

He made a simple knot at the bottom of one pant leg using his teeth to secure it, then tossed it out as far as he could near his other hand holding the bike. It was tricky, but he worked to wedge the knot under the brake lines on the handle bar. Finally he could let go and stretch the jeans out to tie the other leg to a bit of rusty pipe running up the side of the building.

He laid back on the ground. Everything on his body hurt. If that bike ever got fixed, he sure wasn't going to give it back to Brenda, at least not right away.

He rolled over and stood up. The overgrown path led around the side of the building. He followed it and let himself into the warehouse through the steel door. Red was just coming out of the bathroom.

"Hey, Elbow, you weren't here last night. Hope you don't mind but we borrowed some beer from your fridge. What happened to your jeans? Rough night?"

"Great night, rough morning. You doing anything right now? I got the motorbike stuck in the canal and I need some extra muscle to get it out."

"Stuck in the canal? What were you trying to do, jump it?"

"Very funny. Let me find some pants and a board or a pipe and maybe you can help get it out of there. You didn't drink all the beer, did you? Right now, I could use some."

He made a trip to the fridge for beer. First things first. Then he raided the clothing box under his bed and found a pair of sweat pants. It was awfully hot for sweat pants so he rolled them up to the knee.

"How big a pipe do you need, Elbow?" Red was rummaging through the pile of scrap material near the door.

"The damn bike is about three or four feet out. Something strong and long enough we can use as a lever. The canal bottom grabbed onto it pretty good."

They settled on a three-inch sewer pipe that just happened to mysteriously fall off a parked supply truck one night. Red carried the pipe, and Elbow toted a cinder block around back to the canal. He set down the cinder block and they stood there viewing the situation of the jeans tied to the bike handle for a few minutes. "Well, I figure we could use the cinder block as a sort of pivot and put the pipe on top to lever it up like a teeter-totter. What do you think, Red?"

"Yeah, good plan. Is the part sticking up the back or the front?"

"Front."

Together, they slipped the pipe under the handlebars and laid it across the cinder block.

"I only got one strong arm right now. I'll sit on this end of the pipe, and you grab the handle when it comes up and pull it to the edge. OK?"

Red nodded.

Elbow put all his weight on the pipe. The bike resisted, then suddenly released from the bottom. He went crashing to the ground. The bike shot up out of the water followed by a fountain of black sludge. The stench of raw sewage enveloped them.

"God, what's that smell?!"

"Maybe we shouldn't have emptied the Porta-Potty in the canal." Red covered his nose.

"Grab the bike! Grab it before it goes under again!"

Red lunged for the bike and caught the handlebars. "Help me here will you! This thing is heavy and it stinks so bad I think I'm going to hurl!"

Elbow rushed to the rescue. Between them they wrestled it to the side and up onto the path. It dripped puddles of black, toxic waste. They both gasped for fresh air.

"Man, that's foul! What's that thing attached to the back wheel?"

"Snake."

"Snake? You don't mean ... no ... that's the snake that was on TV?"

"The very one."

"And you were on the bike when it crashed into all those cars?"

"Yeah, me and the snake. It was all the snake's fault. I had it all wrapped around it nice and neat, and it just slid off and wham, it caught in the back wheel."

"Half of Miami's in a panic thinking giant snakes are on the prowl attacking cars. You better get rid of that thing quick. Where'd you get the bike anyway?"

"Brenda's."

"That's Brenda's bike? Does she know you have it?"

"We sort of talked about me fixing it."

"Sort of talked? You took it, didn't you! Man, you are one bad dude. You better get the snake off it and fixed in a hurry. Brenda's got some big, hairy friends. People don't mess too much with Brenda."

"Help me wheel it around to the front."

"Hell no, I smell bad enough as it is. And don't leave it under the upstairs windows unless you douse it with a couple gallons of Lysol!"

A fresh collection of flies found the snake and canal sewage coating the bike irresistible. The heat of the day was building. The sooner he got it washed off the better. He hefted the bike up on his shoulder again and almost gagged. It was a struggle, but he managed to drag it around the side of the building to the truck yard.

The shower hose would never stretch out to the yard so he decided to take the bike into the shower to wash it. He unlocked the steel door and propped it open, then steered the bike across the floor to the shower.

Red emerged from the plastic wrapped bathroom wearing a towel around his waist. "Hey, you're not bringing that thing in here are you? You're letting in all the flies! And there's a trail of slime across the floor!"

"I got to get it rinsed off somehow, the hose won't reach outside. I'll clean it up. Did you use up all the hot water?"

"Maybe half a barrel's worth. Serve you right to use cold water. These were my best coveralls. They will probably stink for a year even if I wash them a dozen times."

"Sorry, Red, help yourself to the beer if you want."

The beer offering seemed to soothe Red a bit. "You get in any more trouble with that bike, you just leave me out of it, Okay?"

Elbow headed for the bathroom. He was stiff and sore and tired. When he got to the shower he let the bike crash down on the wooden pallets. He turned the shower head to the 'pulse blast' setting and

let it rip. Most of the black ooze melted away but the lingering odor demanded stronger measures. He grabbed a plastic bucket and emptied every cleaning product he could find into it. He taped Rosita's hair brush to a long stick to scrub all the parts he could reach and gave it another blast of water. Man, he was beat. The beer and the lack of sleep the night before were getting to him, or maybe it was the fumes from the cleaning products. Some of them were not supposed to be mixed together. He turned off the water and left the bike in the shower. If he could just rest for a minute, he would feel better. He headed for his bed, laid down and closed his eyes.

"Hey, you wake up! I got to take shower. You got bike in the shower. Flies everywhere! Wake up!"

Elbow opened his eyes and raised his head. It was Rosita. She was dressed only in a towel, hitting him with a loofah.

"Wake up. You move bike."

"Okay, Okay, I'm up." Elbow stood up. It was almost dark outside. He headed for the shower. He really didn't want to move the damn bike one more time but the shower was shared territory. The flies didn't make it any easier. They were ferocious about the snake guts. Didn't flies sleep at night? He managed to hoist it up on his shoulder and wheel it to the door and out into the truck yard. He dumped it near the building, grabbed some plastic and wrapped it up. It would keep till morning. No sane person would want to go near it.

Rosita was busy loofah-ing it up in the shower, singing with great abandon something about little birds or maybe it was chihuahuas. Elbow's Spanish was a little rusty. What she lacked in pitch she more than made up for in volume.

Somehow he had slept through lunch so he headed for the fridge and found a half gallon of milk. He drank it straight from the carton. There were a few leftover chicken wings that still looked edible. That and a beer would do for dinner. He sat at the table and pondered what to do next. The beer and milk seemed to be having an angry conversation in his stomach. One good belch settled the argument. That was one of the best things about living alone. A person could make all kinds of "personal noises" and there was never anyone to tell you not to. No one got offended if you left dirty dishes in the sink, swore at the TV or slept in your clothes.

Thinking of clothes, it was definitely time to renew the wardrobe. Everything was currently covered with stinking goo or shredded. He rummaged through the clothes box and found his good slacks and

a black tee shirt with ABBA written on the front. Not the most fashionable attire but good enough for a trip to the Salvation Army store.

Now all that was needed was a quick shower. He hoped Rosita hadn't used up all the warm water. Right now he wasn't too particular, he just wanted to get rid of the stink of the canal. The water was lukewarm but felt good. He shaved, slicked back his hair, redid the BandAids and applied a liberal dose of aftershave.

As he left the warehouse, he looked at the bike against the wall. It had only been under the plastic for a short while, but the word was out. Every fly in Miami was having a great time partying at Club Python. Better leave it alone until it got really dark and everything cooled down.

The Salvation Army store was a few blocks away. He took his usual route through back alleys, then across the boulevard into the mall parking lot. The store was at the far end, next to the bowling alley. It had the usual collection of senior men sitting on benches outside, with walkers and canes, waiting for their wives to finish bargain hunting.

Inside, the store was busy. He headed for the men's clothing racks. He checked the sizes of the jeans and inspected likely candidates for holes. There was never a problem with the jeans having that too-new look, but you had to watch out for the holes. He inspected the rack with shirts and found several. With shirts the problem wasn't holes, it was buttons. You had to count the buttons.

He sauntered over to the packages of donated underwear seconds and found some briefs and socks. There was a large table of tennis shoes. He could use a few of those too. Better get several pairs. Once odors like snake guts and blood got hold of shoe linings you couldn't even wash them out.

He was missing a belt. He used the one he had to tie the snake on the bike and it disappeared along with most of the snake. There were some nice ones hanging on the wall. One even had a secret zipper to

hide money or anything else that might need hiding. He checked the size. It might do.

"May I help you?"

Elbow looked up. There was a woman standing behind him. He sized her up in one glance. She had silver-white hair swept up into an elegant coif. Her makeup and nails were professionally done. She obviously didn't buy her clothes at the Salvation Army. The look in her eye was friendly and ... something more.

He smiled back. "Ah, sure. What do you think of this belt?"

"It's a nice belt. Let me help you try it on." She took the belt and leaned toward him, moving her arms around his waist. He got a whiff of her perfume. Expensive. She snugged the belt tighter and took her time threading the leather tongue through the buckle in front. "There, it's ... perfect."

"Thanks." He looked in the mirror against the wall. He caught a glimpse of her giving him the once over from behind, head to toe.

Her smile increased. "You shop here often?"

He smiled back. "No. Just when I need something ... special."

She gave him The Look. He gave her a winning grin. She was a genuine Miami cougar, definitely on the prowl. Elbow figured she had maybe twenty years on him but who's counting. She probably did a shift at the store every once in a while looking for a bit of rough or maybe she trolled there regularly. It didn't matter. He knew The Look when he saw it, and she knew The Smile when she saw it. Simpatico.

He ambled toward the checkout line and reached for a pair of sunglasses on the rotating rack. His old ones ended up under a car in the snake crash incident. He felt naked without them. When it was his turn, he paid a whopping twenty-five bucks for all his selections. He looked around. The silver-haired cougar had disappeared. Oh well, maybe next visit. The lady behind the counter put his things in a black plastic bag and he exited the store.

A large, red, Cadillac convertible pulled up at the curb right in front of him. "Going my way?" the silver-hair asked.

Elbow smiled. He opened the passenger door, threw the plastic bag in the back seat and slid into the red leather interior.

"Better put your seatbelt on, honey. I don't drive slow," she told him.

He fastened himself in and they were off. She seemed to interpret yield signs to mean 'always my turn' and stop signs as mere hints to slow down. The sunglasses perched up against her silver hair were the expensive Dior kind and there were gold rings on most of her fingers.

"What's your name, cowboy?"

"Elbow."

"How'd you get a name like Elbow?" She turned into traffic without the benefit of turn signals. Maybe the red car was bright enough to notice so signaling wasn't necessary.

"Got it as a kid. My brother used to beat me up kind of regular until I jabbed him in the mouth with an elbow one day out of self-defense and sort of dislodged a few teeth. Friends called me 'the Elbow.' The name stuck and reminded my brother not to mess with me. Saved me a lot of bloody noses."

The silver-hair laughed and made a wide turn across several lanes of traffic into a luxe, gated community. She waved a friendly greeting to the attendant at the gate and sped on through down a boulevard lined with tall palm trees and large McMansions. They all sported circular drives and four-car garages. Between the houses on one side of the street, Elbow could see a canal, and on the other side, there were glimpses of the ocean. Posh with a capital P. He wondered which side of the street she lived on, canal or ocean view. The car turned into the circular drive of an ocean view beauty with the required two story

entry, louvered southern shutters and bougainvillea dripping from carefully tended trellises.

"It's not much but it's home," she said with an unapologetic smile.

"Very nice. How many hundred people live here?"

She smiled, amused. "Just me, and the staff. Come on in. I'm thirsty, how about you?"

"Yeah, all that shopping is thirsty work."

She punched in the combination to the front door lock and entered the cool, controlled atmosphere of the marble entrance hall. It was round with two staircases leading up to a single upstairs landing. Elbow wondered why she needed two sets of stairs to go to the same place. Maybe one was the Up and the other was the Down, in case she ever entertained a crowd. She motioned for him to follow her through the ornately decorated living room to the second living room in the back. It faced the lighted pool, outdoor kitchen-grill-patio and a panoramic view of the Atlantic, sparkling in the moonlight. He figured on a clear day you could probably see all the way to Spain.

She walked over to a mahogany-paneled wall and touched one of the panels. It folded back in sections to reveal lighted glass shelves and a collection of liquor that would put the Flaming Flamingo to shame. "What will it be, Elbow? I like margaritas when it's hot. How about you?"

"Yeah, margaritas sound great." He hoped it would be a straight tequila margarita, not one of those fruity, strawberry things. It seemed impolite to ask for anything as simple as a beer with an extravaganza of a bar like that shining in front of him. It was a thing to behold. She busied herself whipping up margaritas.

"So, what's your name?" He asked.

"Guess."

"Well, something exotic maybe, like Esmeralda or Jacqueline."

"No," she laughed, then ran her manicured fingernails across the front of his shirt. "It's ... Abba!"

He looked at his shirt and laughed. She handed him the margarita and touched her glass to his. There it was again, The Look. He gazed at her over the salt on the rim of his glass as he took a sip. This promised to be the start of a beautiful friendship.

Elbow rolled over in the giant bed. Sun filtered gently through the palm trees and silk curtains. The Atlantic Ocean shimmered in the distance. Man, this was one swank house. The bedroom alone was big enough to host tennis matches. He was a little too preoccupied the night before to check out the bathroom but he would bet his last beer it was wall to wall marble with gold faucets.

His head buzzed from the margaritas and other beverages the night before. Abba certainly knew her way around the well-stocked bar. She also knew her way around more than the bar. The bed was one of those super-sized ones and they used every square inch of it. She had a very healthy appetite, not that he minded of course, but perhaps she was just a little bit out of his league. She was maybe a barracuda rather than a cougar.

He got himself vertical without too much trouble and found the bathroom. He would have won the beer bet. It was an extravaganza of marble and there were porcelain fixtures with gold trim too. It was almost hard to pee into the gold rimmed toilet.

Someone had brought up the black plastic bag with his Salvation Army wardrobe and put it in the bathroom. Elbow showered. He wondered what the superrich used for soap and shampoo. He tried one of the elegant bottles on the shower shelf. He was engulfed in suds which, he had to admit, did an admirable job of 'cleansing and hydration.' He dried off and searched for a comb. His hair was "volumized", according to the label on the shower bottle. It needed a firm hand to slick it back into something that didn't resemble Shirley Temple.

He searched for toothpaste, found it and applied it to his finger to give his teeth a rub. A quick rinse with water and a polish to the front teeth with a towel completed the routine. His face could have used a

razor but it wasn't bad with a fashionable two-day stubble. None of the wounds needed retreads.

He selected a new shirt and underwear from the plastic bag and removed the tags. The blue shirt matched his eyes. The slacks he had on yesterday would do. Put on the sunglasses and he was good to go.

He followed the long hallway to the double stairway. They came up the right one last night so he chose the left one to go down today. He didn't want to get ticketed for going against traffic on the wrong stairs. He wandered out onto the patio to see what the ocean was doing. The sun was shining, seagulls were flying and Abba was doing laps in the pool. She finished a lap and stopped at the edge.

"Good morning, hotshot, want some breakfast?"

"Coffee maybe. Thanks."

She walked up the steps out of the pool. Elbow slid admiring eyes up and down her leopard-print swimsuit and well-tended body. Either she was an Olympic athlete or she had a lot of work done. She noticed and smiled. He brought her a towel and patted her shoulders dry. She tied a gauzy cover up over one shoulder and slipped into high heeled sandals. He followed her into the kitchen which probably rivaled ones on cruise ships with every appliance known to man.

"Two coffees please, Raymond."

"Yes, madam."

Elbow watched as Raymond, the butler, robotically operated the deluxe coffee setup and produced two perfect cups of coffee, then served them at the patio table along with madam's morning orange juice. He noticed the man never looked at him once. He felt invisible, even disposable. Raymond had evidently seen it all before. Madam was having another little fling and it was never any of his business.

Still, it had been a great night and touring the la-la land of the rich had been a treat. Abba was quite a gal. He wondered how long her taste for chili dogs would last before she moved on to filet mignon.

Whatever. He would ride it out just to see. The Ritz sure beat the crusty warehouse anytime.

"I thought maybe we should go to the race track this afternoon. Do you have a sport jacket?" Abba asked.

Elbow was amused and smiled. "No, I usually stand at the rail. Jackets aren't required."

She smiled back. "I'll have Raymond pick something out for you. Some of my late husband's things might fit you."

"What did your late husband do, if you don't mind me asking?"

She hesitated before answering. "... Imports."

Imports could mean anything from cars to drugs or gun running. Better not press it. Whatever it was, it made a bundle of cash and maybe it was the reason he was her <u>late</u> husband. Better not go there. She wanted to go to the track. The day was looking more promising every minute.

Raymond was summoned and asked to find something to fit. Elbow followed the butler on another tour through the house, this time to a distant bedroom. The closet was huge. After selecting a fashionable blue sport coat to compliment Elbow's shirt, Raymond slipped it on his shoulders without once looking him in the eye or talking. Raymond was a snob. The jacket fit like a glove.

Next, a hat was selected from the collection on the top shelf. A genuine Panama that fit perfectly too. Elbow cocked the hat at an angle and viewed himself in the large, three way mirror at the end of the closet. He admired the dude looking back at him. Now if he didn't forget to remove the hat in the presence of the ladies, he just might pull off the look. The butler made a short bow to usher him out of the closet and back down stairs. Good thing there was a guide. A trail of bread crumbs would have been needed to find the way back.

Abba had gone upstairs to dress so Elbow wandered around the patio and down to the wall at the edge of the ocean. The small bit of sand that served as a beach was as pristine as the clipped hedges and

perfectly cut grass. The grounds crew that tended Bush Gardens must be employed there too. All that perfection made him uneasy. Maybe Abba had the same problem and shopped the Salvation Army to relieve the monotony.

Then Elbow spotted him, a heavy, muscled dude standing under a tree at the other end of the beach, watching him. Abba had a watch dog in a suit and sunglasses. Maybe she wanted to make sure nobody stole sand from the beach, but the guy was definitely paid muscle. Elbow reminded himself to act casual.

An hour later, Abba appeared on the patio dressed in a dazzling red dress and matching red sun hat. Elbow saw her from the other end of the lawn as she motioned him to come. He obeyed. She nodded approval of the new and improved Elbow. He nodded approval of anything red. On her it looked spectacular.

She handed him her toy poodle and went off to give instructions to the butler. Elbow looked at the poodle. The poodle looked at him and bared its teeth. Was it smiling or planning to rip off his lip? What was it with some people and animals, just bad vibes? Thank God it wasn't a cockatoo. Elbow managed a polite smile as a show of goodwill to the poodle. The dog gave him a sniff and kept a wary eye in his direction. Abba returned from the kitchen and gave the poodle a nuzzling kiss. It wagged its tail vigorously in Elbow's armpit.

"We can have lunch at the track." Abba walked toward to the front door. Elbow surmised he was to follow behind as the official poodle carrier. It might be worth a free lunch.

A chauffeured Rolls was waiting outside the front door. The chauffeur opened the door for them. Abba entered first and took the seat next to the door. Evidently she didn't slide. Elbow walked around to the other side and did his own door opening. The muscle suit joined them and sat in the front passenger seat with the chauffeur. The poodle took its usual spot in the middle next to Abba, and they were off to the races.

The improved weather brought out the crowds for the afternoon racing action. Abba headed straight for the upper grandstand clubhouse. The doorman gave them a salute and opened the door for her. She was a regular. No one asked for an ID. They rode the elevator together to the top floor along with the bodyguard and stepped out into a dazzling world of upper crust privileges. The manager came at them with a beaming smile and kissed Abba on both cheeks.

"This is Mr. .. Elbow," Abba told him.

"Ah, Mr. El Beau, welcome," the manager extended his hand. "Your table is ready, Mrs. Mancozzi. Jules will be your waiter today. Enjoy the races." He personally escorted them to a table in the front row, against the glass, overlooking the finish line. It was high above the teaming masses. Abba settled in and gave the poodle its own chair. Jules appeared immediately to take drink orders, then scurried away.

"Mr. El Beau," Abba teased. "What _is_ your last name?"

" ... Smith."

Abba laughed. "Well, Mr. _Smith_, you look like a man who might know something about horse races. Who do you favor in the first race?"

It seemed like a challenge. Elbow took the racing form provided on the table and scanned the first race offerings. Several horses might be good starters. "Ella's Dream or Mickey Moe in the first," he announced.

Abba looked at the list. "Really! They're not the favorites. Wonder boy seems like a good name. Want to make a wager?"

"I seem to have left my other wallet in the Salvation Army bag."

She laughed again. He could see there was no pretense between them. She was a filthy rich matron and he was just Elbow, along for the ride, sporting a black eye and second-hand clothes.

She opened her large, red handbag and handed him two crisp Benjamins. "You pick yours and put a bet on Wonder Boy for me. We'll see who wins."

He did as he was told. The bodyguard suddenly reappeared and followed him into the elevator. The man was huge. His bulk reflected in the mirrored walls and seemed to take up most of the space. Even behind the sunglasses, the guy never blinked once. His head was shaved, his expression carved in stone, and there was an extra bulge under his arm that was a different kind of muscle. Elbow tried to avoid his gaze and act nonchalant so he didn't sweat too much.

The elevator doors opened and Elbow headed for the familiar betting windows. He placed the bets, took the slips and headed back to the elevators.

"Elbow, you old son of a gun!"

It was Bobby Mac, good old Bobby Mac, who got into a bar fight with him one night, then ran away and left him to fend for himself against two rubes from Fort Lauderdale. "Hey Bobby, how's tricks?"

"Pretty fine, pretty fine. Say, you couldn't lend me a fiver, could you? I'm a little flat right now and I got a hot tip in the third."

"Sorry, I'm fresh out," Elbow said. It wasn't true. His pocket still held twelve dollars and thirty-six cents, but Bobby was never going to see any of it. The bar fight memory was still fresh. Elbow continued on to the Top Deck elevators with his bulky sidekick in tow and was ushered right through by the attendant. He turned and gave Bobby a wide grin as the elevator doors started to close. Bobby's face dropped. Elbow enjoyed that. Payback was always sweet.

He returned to the table and presented Abba with the betting slips. Their drinks had arrived. Abba still favored Margaritas and Elbow liked beer on racetrack days. Jules attentively took their lunch orders.

Elbow scanned the crowd as the Upper Deck restaurant filled with avid, monied, race goers. There were older tycoons sporting young beauties on their arms and smart-aleck, playboy wannabes with too much cash and time to spend it on women dressed in chic dresses and sunglasses. It was a bit of an upper crust meat market, everyone giving everyone else the eye. Several men showed up at Abba's table to chat. Elbow had plenty of time to study them since they barely gave him a glance.

One or two of them he recognized. They were not the kind of men you would want to owe money to or meet in a dark alley. Then it hit him. Her last name was Mancozzi. Oh hell, that Mancozzi. No wonder she lived in a mansion. Her husband was rumored to run several import rackets. That explained the muscle suit with the bulge

under his arm. Elbow twitched. His skin suddenly itched wearing the late Mr. Mancozzi's sport coat.

Abba seemed nice enough but you never knew. Mixing with that crowd was a little like running with the bulls in Spain. Dangerous and stupid. Project the wrong attitude, and you might get popped for looking at somebody the wrong way. As pleasant as it was to drink margaritas and play around in a king-sized bed, maybe it was time to look for an exit strategy.

Jules appeared with a crab Louis salad for Abba and the nachos grande for Elbow. He picked at the chips and drank another beer while Abba fed small crab tidbits to the poodle.

Horses for the first race started their parade past the grandstand to the starting gates. Abba's horse, Wonder Boy, held the enviable, first starting position. Elbow's pick, Mickey Moe, was four gates farther out. Abba retrieved binoculars from her handbag and inspected the field. Wonder Boy was calm on his way to the gate, but Mickey Moe danced in circles. She gave Elbow a knowing smile. Mickey would probably dance in the gate too and be last one out at the bell. Elbow tried to tell himself it was just a horse race and the bet was with someone else's play money, but he suddenly wished Mickey Moe would beat the hell out of the field and run like his tail was on fire.

The gate shut on the last horse. All eyes riveted on the track. The bell rang. The gates flew open. The pent up horses charged out. Wonder Boy made a nice start along the rail joined by two of the favorites. Mickey Moe had some catching up to do on the outside but held his own in the middle of the pack. The field thundered past the grandstands. It was a full mile and anything could happen. The leaders put a small distance between themselves and the jumble of horses in the rear. At the first turn, the pack began to spread out a bit. There was a little breathing room to run without interference and Mickey Moe moved to close the gap.

Abba hugged the glass with her binoculars. "Come on, Wonder Boy, come on!"

Elbow's eyes were on the opening opportunities as the field rounded the second turn. The front-runners stayed in a tight group, trying their best to stay in the lead, expending at lot of energy. Mickey Moe made a small gain through the back stretch to join them. There was no room to pass along the rail, so the jockey took him to the outside as they rounded the third turn.

Elbow groaned internally. Did Mickey have it in him to go the extra distance? With open track in front of him, the horse found an extra gear and by the time they entered the home stretch it was a three-way race to the finish line. It would be close. The jockey showed Mickey the tip of his whip and that was all it took to stretch past and win by a nose. Elbow clapped his hands.

Abba put down her binoculars. Wonder Boy finished third. Close, but no cigar. "Okay, Mr. Smith, fair's fair." She handed him the winning betting slip. "You won. You get to collect your winnings, but when you come back, you'll have to tell me your secret."

"It's no secret. First look at the wins and speed for the horses. Take the best, maybe look at the odds, then bet the jockeys. It's not fool

proof, but good jockeys can make a difference, like today with that move to the outside and just a flick of the whip near the finish. Anyway, it sure beats betting the cutest name."

"I have a feeling there's more to you than I suspected."

Elbow winked. "I play a mean game of pool too. A sure sign of a misspent youth."

Abba smiled. Somewhere under that well groomed exterior there was a hint of another misspent youth. "While you're there, who do you favor in the second?" She asked.

He grinned. She was a fast learner. The track wouldn't make much money on her today.

The ride back to the ocean villa in the Rolls was downright joyful. Abba liked to win. Elbow didn't mind being on the receiving end of the betting bounty either. It was far more fun betting someone else's Benjamins than his own fivers, especially when the planets aligned and the ponies cooperated. Abba was in a very good mood. He wondered what her mood would be if she lost. Better not think about that now, just enjoy the ride. Abba disappeared upstairs to shower and change before dinner. Evidently all that betting and winning was gritty work.

Elbow asked the butler for a beer and made himself comfy on the patio. He mentally counted his haul from the track. No need to work for beer money for quite a long while. Maybe even pay someone to deal with the snake carcass and fix the bike. By now, the snake must be reduced to mush after fragrantly marinating under plastic in hot sun all day. The flies were probably sending out e-mails to cousins in Georgia to join the party.

A cool breeze drifted onto the patio from the ocean. Palm trees swayed and filtered the sun, making dancing patterns on the stone floor. Elbow put his feet up on the chair opposite and leaned back. This was heaven, Miami style.

A large figure suddenly loomed above him, blocking out the sun. "Enjoying the air ... Mr. .. Smith?"

Elbow looked up. It was the muscle suit, bigger than life. The behemoth could actually speak.

"Yeah, nice day."

"You might not want to get too comfy, sir. Ms. Abba's guests usually don't stay too long, if you know what I mean."

"Yeah, I figured that out already. Thanks."

"Just a friendly suggestion."

"Sure. I know when to move along."

"Tomorrow morning might be good. I can arrange for a car."

"Yeah, thanks."

The suit moved off to resume his watch from the underbrush or wherever he did his lurking. It was a polite enough conversation but a little scary. Were those Abba's instructions or instructions to the staff from the late Mr. Mancozzi? Maybe the muscle brain invented it on his own. Whatever. It was time to come down from the clouds and go back to reality. Too much rarified air was bad for your health and Abba's air was crowded with some pretty heavy breathers. No need to risk overhearing private conversations or get caught in crossfire.

Abba made an appearance wearing a gauzy, flowered caftan over skin- tight, white leather jeans. Not every cougar could pull that off, but on her it looked downright comfortable and sexy. She headed for the expansive bar and had the butler tend to margaritas. Elbow helped her with a chair on the patio and they sat enjoying the early evening as the sun set and the sky settled into dusk.

He broached the subject of leaving. "It sure has been nice, Abba, but I don't want to wear out my welcome. Maybe I should run along tonight or tomorrow morning."

"No."

It was a definite no, more a command than a request. Elbow began to feel a little uneasy. "It's been a great time, but you maybe have other things to do .. like beating the odds at the track or helping out at the Salvation Army. I don't want to be in your way."

"No."

He tried to keep it friendly. "I got some things I need to do too. A friend wants me to fix a motorbike. I sort of promised."

She looked at him over the top of her margarita. "You can stay here a little longer and keep me company. I get mighty lonely rattling around this big, old house all by myself. I like you. You aren't like those flashy guys who just want to dip into my checking account or some of my late husband's friends who think I'm some dumb bimbo they can

schmooze up to and get let in on the business. I go where I want and I do what I want."

"I'm a free spirited kind of guy too. We've had some laughs and bet the ponies, but .."

"No buts. Stay for dinner and we'll talk, OK? You thirsty, honey? The bar is open. Let me refresh that beer for you." She walked off. End of conversation.

Elbow was beginning to feel trapped. He always enjoyed being free to come and go as he pleased. This was like being in a cage. Sure, it was a gold plated cage, but it was still a cage if the door didn't swing open. Carrying poodles and playing Don Juan to matrons wasn't exactly his style, even if it included free beer and betting money in his pocket.

Weaseling out of relationships had never been hard, but this one presented a few problems. First there was the house. It was huge. A guy could end up wandering around for days looking for an exit door before anyone found him. It would be even harder in the dark. Then there was the problem of finding the front gate, wherever that was. This was a fancier part of town, pretty far from home. A fellow walking down the street in this neighborhood, late at night, carrying a big plastic bag, would attract attention, maybe a couple of squad cars. He was stuck. The luxe life was losing its luster. Time to plan an escape.

For some reason the muscle suit was keen to get rid of him. Maybe that could be parlayed into a quick exit. While Abba was busy getting the beer and a retread on her margarita, Elbow wandered out onto the lawn. The suit was never far away. As soon as he neared the sea wall, the suit materialized.

"Ah, I was wondering," Elbow started.

"Yes, Mr. Smith."

"I was thinking about your offer of a ride, maybe tonight?"

The man turned his stone face to look at the house, then slowly turned back to look at Elbow. "Tomorrow morning, early."

"How early is early?"

"Five a.m."

"Five a.m.? Not even the palmetto bugs get up that early."

There was no change in the man's expression. It was take it or leave it.

"Okay then. Where do I go?"

"I'll find you. And it would be a good idea not to mention it to Mrs. Mancozzi." He turned and seemed to melt back into the landscaping.

Elbow made his way back to the patio. Five a.m.? Really? Was it that hard to leave Abba's company? What was all the cloak and dagger stuff about? This was beginning to feel like a bad, B movie plot. There should be spooky music so you knew when the good guy was going to get hit over the head or shot at.

Abba was back on the patio with drinks. "What were you doing out there, honey? It's getting dark."

Elbow tried to stay casual. "Just checking out the ocean. There's a nice moon rising. I don't get to see much moon or ocean where I live."

"Where's that?"

Oh God, she was asking questions. It was a bad sign when they started asking questions. No way was he going to tell her where he lived. "My place is a dump in a rough neighborhood. It's really a squat I share with two other people. It kind of matches my Salvation Army wardrobe." He smiled.

She smiled back. "Sometimes I wish I lived in just a simple place with lots going on around me. Then I'd be free. Money's a drag sometimes."

"Yeah, It's a drag if you don't have it too." Why did the rich always whine about how complicated their lives were and yearn for the simple life. They could just buy it.

Elbow turned over on the silk sheets and looked at the ceiling in the dark. After a string of margaritas at dinner, Abba got very clingy. There was really no way to extricate himself other than using chloroform, so they ended up in bed again. I mean when a woman comes at you wearing tight, leather jeans and not too much else, it's a little hard to deny basic urges and say no. Beyond that, she was mighty fine in bed, a bit demanding perhaps, but mighty fine.

He looked at his watch again. 4:35. The last time he looked it was 4:32. Time to get up and get dressed. He was pretty careful about shedding his clothes in a pile next to the bed the night before so they wouldn't end up scattered. He slowly moved to the edge of the bed and put both feet on the floor. So far so good. Abba was sleeping next to him, snoring slightly.

The moon still shined bright enough so he could sort out things on the floor. The snoring stopped. He froze. The sheets moved and Abba turned over. He waited. After a couple of minutes her breathing was shallow and regular again. It felt safe enough to move. He put on his pants, socks and shoes and slipped into his shirt. He could button it later. He negotiated the bedroom by moonlight to retrieve his bag of clothes from the bathroom. It was bulky and he had to be doubly careful not to knock anything over on his way to the hallway door.

He turned the door handle to open the door. It clicked. He froze again. Abba's breathing didn't change. The door opened silently and Elbow moved through it into the hallway. He breathed a sigh of relief. He tip-toed a few steps away and buttoned his shirt. When he went to tuck it into his slacks, panic set in.

He frantically checked his pockets. His wallet was missing with all that beautiful horse racing cash. It probably slipped out of his pocket next to the bed. He stood there for a minute to think. Oh hell, he

would have to go back in to get it. He didn't want to. It was a risk, but he couldn't ever remember having that much cash.

He took a deep breath and turned the door handle again. The door opened a crack. Everything was still quiet. He got down on his hands and knees to crawl across the carpet toward the bed, his hands reaching in every direction for the wallet. As he neared the bed, Abba moved again, rolling over closer to his side of the bed. He flattened himself on the floor and waited. He dared to raise his eyes above the top of the mattress to take a look. She was sleeping again only inches from the side of the bed.

He checked every inch of floor next to the bed and under the bed with his hands. No wallet. He looked at the long expanse of carpet between the bed and the bathroom. Was that a dark shape near the chair leg, way over there by the bathroom door? He crawled to it, still checking the floor with sweeping motions of his hands. He touched it. Come to papa! It was the wallet! He kissed it. The only thing left to do was keep quiet and make it to the door. He stayed on all fours, crawling past the bed and out the door into the hall.

He ran into a large pair of shoes. He looked up. It was the muscle suit who briefly lit a small flashlight beam in his face and motioned him to stand up and be quiet. Elbow grabbed the plastic bag of clothes and followed the suit down the hall to the stairs. The muscle suit grabbed his arm at the bottom of the stairs, and pulled him in a quick left turn to a narrow back hallway.

The suit stopped suddenly and pressed them both against the wall. A small sliver of light showed under a door to the right. Someone coughed. They heard water running. Several minutes later the light went out, and they hurried past the door. At the end of the hallway was another, larger door. The suit touched a few buttons on the box next to the door to unlock and disarm it, and they stepped outside into the cool, humid air of morning. The sky was just starting to show a hint of pink in the east.

They continued on across a freshly watered patch of lawn to the back of the garage. The suit unlocked the door with a key and they entered. It was huge. All the cars were lined up, Abba's red convertible, the Rolls, a couple of Maseratis, and a Porsche. Abba liked her cars fast and deluxe. The chauffeur stepped out of the shadows and nodded to the suit. He motioned them to the back of the Rolls and opened the trunk. "Get in."

Elbow protested. "What? No way! Can't I just lay down in the back seat?"

"Quiet! You want to bring the house down on us?"

They motioned for him to get in. Elbow did as he was told. They tossed the plastic bag in with him and closed the trunk. This was getting weird. Both front car doors opened and he felt the two men get in the car. He heard the soft whirring of the garage door opener. He rolled slightly in the trunk as the car backed out, turned and started down the driveway. The car slowed. He figured they must be at the front gate. He felt the car turn right.

Then it dawned on him. They never asked where he lived. Where the hell were they taking him? He heard laughter. Wow, was he ever a first class idiot! It was all a big joke on him. They had him coming and going. They rousted him out of bed at an unholy hour, put the fear of God into him with all the cloak and dagger nonsense and stuffed him in a car trunk. They were probably going to dump him somewhere in the Everglades and laugh all the way back.

How could he get out of the trunk? His mind raced. This was a late model Rolls. Maybe there was a safety trunk latch somewhere. His fingers frantically traced the interior of the trunk lid in the dark. There, that small, plastic square thing in the middle. That must be it.

Now, where were they? Elbow could feel the car get up to speed and stop occasionally. They were traveling along the boulevard. How many times did they stop? He started to count. It could give him a rough idea of where he was. The car also turned several times and went

up and down over canal bridges. His mental picture of where they were was scrambled. Damn, they could be anywhere.

The car slowed and stopped. Both front doors opened and the men got out. He could hear cars and traffic. Elbow found the equipment storage panel in the trunk, managed to open it and fumbled around for the tire iron. He braced himself for the trunk opening. It didn't. What was going on?

After a few minutes, he pressed the small button. The trunk popped open a crack. He peered out. Damn! The car was in the parking lot of a pancake house! The two guys were inside having breakfast while he roasted in the trunk! Time to exit the charade. He raised the trunk lid slowly and climbed out with the plastic bag and the tire iron. He checked his pocket for the wallet and closed the trunk behind him. He kept a low profile along the side of the car. It was time for a little payback.

He casually looked around to make sure no one was watching, then squatted down next to the tires on the right side of the car, away from the restaurant windows. He removed the air valve caps and threw them in the shrubbery. He let air out of both tires. That should do it. The car should have a nice lean to the right to keep them busy for a while. He buried the tire iron in the mulch in front of the car for good measure.

He took refuge in the landscaping, stood up and looked around. He suddenly knew where he was. Five or six blocks down the next street was the Flaming Flamingo. He was home. The laughing boys had accidentally brought him to the right neighborhood. He knew all the alleys and short cuts. No trouble hiding if they finally got their fancy car mobile again and decided to come looking for him. Besides, it wasn't exactly the right neighborhood to go looking for someone in a Roller. They might think twice about getting Abba's car stripped of the wheels and fancy upholstery.

He turned, gave the car a selected finger salute and walked away. He was free. Free from the trunk, free from the muscle suit and even free

from Abba. He would miss the ocean and maybe the margaritas, but freedom was a beautiful thing.

Elbow hurried along the street, casting a glance behind every once in a while to make sure the laughing boys were not in sight. You could never be too careful with guys who played with guns and had a warped sense of humor. He slowed down a bit as he passed the Flaming Flamingo. It wasn't open that early in the morning. He hardly recognized it. At night, the lights cast their hot pink glow on the street so you didn't notice the gum and other mess on the sidewalk and the bottles piled up in the alley.

He turned into the shortcut through the alley at the corner and headed for the back of Juan's Mexican Restaurant. It wasn't open yet either, but the smell of tacos and hot peppers filled the air for almost a block in all directions. There was yelling coming from behind the fence. Juan was leaning out the back door shouting, threatening to hit a young girl with a large spoon. She was crying. When Juan saw Elbow, he ducked back inside and slammed the door. The girl collapsed on the ground, sobbing. She was wearing a flowered dress and her hair was arranged in a long braid down her back. She didn't look like one of the waitresses.

"You all right?" Elbow asked.

She looked up at him with big brown eyes full of tears. A stream of unintelligible Spanish words babbled out of her. Elbow's Spanish was very rusty. He couldn't understand a single word. He helped her to stand and motioned for her to sit on a small orange crate near the dumpster. The words babbled on.

Elbow knocked on the back door of the restaurant. Pedro stuck his head out and rapidly looked behind to make sure the boss, Juan, wasn't in the kitchen. Elbow knew him. They had raised a few libations together at the Flamingo.

"Hey, Pedro, what's going on. Why's the girl sitting there crying?"

"Juan is pretty mad. He don't want. He send her back. She got no ID, no nothing."

"How old is she anyway? She looks like she's just a kid."

"Yeah, maybe sixteen, maybe fifteen." Pedro looked behind him again. "Got to go. Got to chop lettuce or boss gets mad. Bye." He waved to the girl and closed the door.

What did Juan do, order her through a catalog and then just toss her out? Juan was a pig. Poor kid. Rosita might be able to do something with her. At least she could get the straight story out of her. Rosita maybe knew some people who could get her a green card or something. He motioned for her to stand up and follow him. The girl obeyed, following three feet behind, her sandals flopping on the pavement. She hurried to catch up and tugged at the plastic bag.

"Hey, what do you think you're doing?"

She motioned to let her to carry it. She didn't seem the type to steal it. There wasn't too much in it that was valuable anyway. He let her have it. She put it on her back and followed along at his heels. He led her through a few back alleys, looking back every once in a while to see if she was still with him.

At last, they entered the truck yard next to the warehouse. He stopped to look at the motorbike that had been marinating in the hot sun for several days under the plastic. The girl's eyes got wide at the sight of all the flies and maggots. Elbow opened the warehouse door and motioned for her to enter. She timidly obeyed. He motioned again for her to follow him up the stairs to Red and Rosita's digs, but the girl stood frozen, staring at the sheets of plastic hanging up around the rusty, grimy interior.

Elbow yelled up the stairs. "Hey, Rosita, anybody home? I got someone here I want you to meet." He hoped Rosita was at least half dressed. The girl was scared enough as it was.

Rosita appeared at the top of the stairs wearing a pink sweat suit with a red scarf tied around her hair. "What you want, Elbow? I cleaning Pepito's cage."

"I got someone here you need to talk to. Juan was tossing her out of the back of the restaurant. She doesn't speak any English. Maybe you can understand what she's saying."

Rosita came down the stairs and spoke a few words of Spanish to her. The girl's face lit up with a smile bright enough to illuminate half of Miami. She hugged Rosita. Rosita managed to get her to sit at the card table. The girl grabbed her hand and wouldn't let go.

"Elbow, you get me beer and some soda for Carmen."

"That's her name, Carmen?"

"Yeah, you get drinks."

"Anything else while you're ordering me around?"

"You tell Red come down and bring Pepitto."

He delivered the soda and beer and headed for the stairs to the upstairs room. As soon as he entered, Pepitto unleashed a barrage of noise in his direction. Evidently cockatoos had long memories. Elbow gave it the evil eye stare. The bird returned the favor with a quick head jerk and snapped its beak a few times. He gave the bird a wide detour.

Red was just putting the finishing details on his jade green cushion painting of Rosita. "Hey Elbow, you've been gone for two nights. Hope you don't mind but we borrowed some beer from the fridge. Where have you been, in jail?"

"No, I'll tell you about it sometime when I get good and drunk. Rosita is downstairs with a girl Juan was throwing out the back of his restaurant. She wants you to go down and bring the winged wonder here with you."

Elbow left before Red managed to get the bird to perch on his shoulder for the trip down the stairs. When Carmen saw the bird she smiled and caressed it with little cooing words. The bird cooed right

back and gave her a full, preening salute with a raised comb and kisses with its beak and white tongue.

"Damn cheeky bird," Elbow muttered.

Rosita beamed. "See, he like her. She stay. You fix nice place for her."

Elbow backed away. "What? Oh no, not me. You find her a place. Maybe you can get her a work permit or something and she can find her own place."

"She nice. Juan pay father money for to marry her. But Juan, he say she too young, too small to work. But she sixteen, almost. That a good age in Mexico, but no here. Juan not like. Kick her out. Many brothers and sisters at home. Father already takes money. She can no go home. I see Juan, I kill him."

Elbow thought she just might do that. "Maybe you can get her a work permit or something and she can find a place to stay."

"She stay here. You fix nice room for her. She don't need much.I know a guy. Maybe he get her papers, maybe. You fix."

Elbow protested. "Rosita, I got things to do. I got to fix the bike. Maybe she could stay with you upstairs."

"No room. You bring her here, you fix. She stay! You fix!" With that, Rosita took Pepitto and walked back up the stairs.

Red shrugged. "Rosita has spoken."

Elbow looked at Carmen and turned to go into his private plastic draped domain, his inner sanctum, his bedroom. It was great to be home again. Maybe it wasn't as lush and fancy as Abba's posh mansion, but it was his and he could come and go as he pleased. Being tied down just wasn't his style. A guy's got to live in his own clothes and feel free.

Elbow changed into jeans and put the rest of his Salvation Army duds away in the box under the Styrofoam bed, then raided the fridge for a cold beer. Ah, breakfast. He wandered out into the open warehouse. Carmen was still sitting at the table, waiting patiently. He stepped out into the truck yard to inspect the motorbike that was still cooking in the hot sun under the plastic cover. Carmen followed closely behind.

By now the snake was reduced to a gelatinous mash covered in maggots. He had to do it sometime. He had to rip off the plastic and get on with cleaning up the bike. Gingerly gripping one corner of the plastic, he ran as fast as he could to the other end of the truck yard. Parts of snake goo clung to the plastic along with maggots and flies. The stench was overwhelming. Carmen turned away and held her nose. Elbow gasped for air, then folded the plastic over on itself to help contain the smell. Elbow's breakfast beer was trying to decide whether to stay down or come up. Man, that was one mean, nasty snake. Even dead, it was getting its revenge.

He picked up a long pipe and from a safe distance of twelve feet started poking the mush of snake still embedded around the rear bike wheel. It oozed down onto the worn tarmac in liquid chunks releasing more foul odors. He toughed it out until most of the snake was gone then moved the bike to a less odorous spot to inspect it.

Carmen squatted down next to him and watched him inspect the damage.. The back wheel was a definitely warped. As long as the gears were okay, it was an easy fix. The wheel was just a smaller, thicker

version of a bicycle tire. The spokes could be tightened and adjusted to bring it back in shape. Piece of cake. No problem. What could go wrong?

Carmen looked at him expectantly. She said something in Spanish. Having no clue what she said, he just smiled and nodded his head. He headed into the warehouse to retrieve a bucket and a brush with something to wash down the bike. Carmen was right at his heels. As soon as he filled up the bucket she wanted to take it out of his hand to carry it.

"Okay, okay, you can carry it, but don't get anything in here wet. Listen to me, I'm talking to her as if she actually understands English."

Carmen smiled and proceeded to slosh water from the heavy bucket all the way to the door. Elbow rolled his eyes and followed the trail of water out the door. She wrapped her dress around her legs and squatted down next to the bike, attacking the back wheel enthusiastically with the soapy brush.

"Easy, easy. Watch the paint!"

Carmen looked up, suddenly afraid she was doing something wrong. He made motions with his hands to indicate a more gentle approach. She made the same gentle motions.

"Good, Good. *Bueno.*"

Carmen smiled up at him, her brown eyes glowing. Elbow had seen that look before, the kind of look that says unconditional admiration, only it was on the face of a golden retriever. This was not a good thing. Sure the kid was in a tight spot, alone in a strange place, and he had been kind of nice to her, but he didn't need a golden retriever. Maybe Rosita could explain how things were.

Elbow removed the wheel from the back of the bike while Carmen watched his every move. She seemed to instinctively know when he needed a certain tool or when to hold the bike still. Elbow sensed she had either watched or helped someone do it before. He brought the wheel inside to wash it more thoroughly with the shower hose. Carmen took over and gave the wheel another good scrub. It was a little tight in the shower so he left her to it.

He wandered into the kitchen area and helped himself to another beer and some Cocoa Puffs. The box was almost empty. Time to make a beer and food run to the store. He retrieved the 'borrowed' shopping cart from the side of the warehouse and started to wheel it toward the alley. Carmen appeared immediately and wanted to push it for him. It had an annoying, wonky wheel so he let her.

She followed along behind, looking at everything. He laughed. The alley wasn't the best Miami had to offer, but to her it must all be new and interesting. They turned at the end, crossed the parking lot and entered the store.

Just inside the door, Carmen stood still. Her eyes grew wide at the varieties of food in front of her. Elbow continued on to the liquor department to load up on his beverage of choice. Carmen scurried to help. Twelve-packs of beer were no problem for her. She was made of sturdy stuff and filled the bottom of the cart with several cartons.

She spotted the racks of taco chips and put several bags in the cart. Elbow took them out and she put them back in. She was a whirlwind. He couldn't stop her. She added two packages of ground beef, tomato sauce, cheese and a small bag of onions. He quickly grabbed a couple of boxes of cereal and headed for the checkout isle before she could add anything else.

"Well, hello there, Elbow, who's your new sidekick?" Chirped Devonne behind the counter.

"Carmen. Just here for a visit," Elbow lied.

"Rosita's sister?"

"More like a cousin or something."

"She's cute."

Carmen eyed the 'tempt and tease' selection of chocolate bars next to the checkout station. She timidly reached up, smiled at Elbow and put two Hersey bars on the counter.

"And hungry, evidently," Elbow hurried to pay. He put everything back in the cart and made a fast exit.

Carmen sang a little song as she pushed the full shopping cart along the alley. She did a sort of dance and even twirled around once. Elbow began to wonder just how old she really was, fifteen, sixteen, thirteen? It was hard to tell with that braid and her petite size.

When they returned to the warehouse, Carmen busied herself in the kitchen area, cleaning. Cleaning wasn't Elbow's thing so he enjoyed another beer. He wheeled the bike tire out into the truck yard again to work on it. It was tricky, but he managed to straighten the spokes and tighten the alignment so the tire looked pretty even. It took the rest of the afternoon to mount it back on the bike, apply grease and get the bike running. Mission accomplished but he was covered in oily grit.

He entered the bathroom to freshen up and was almost bowled over. Someone had committed a neatness. The smell of Lysol was overwhelming. The shower stall and sink sparkled. The inside of the Porta-Potty looked almost sanitary. The grunge had actually disappeared from the floor and you could see the concrete. Either Carmen had cleaned it or the health department had finally condemned the place and sent in a team of cleaners in hazmat suits with power washers.

Carmen had been busy in the kitchen, cleaning that too. A tiny island of shining concrete surrounded the card table, the mismatched shelves with the microwave ,and the refrigerator that served as the kitchen. Red and Rosita were sitting at the card table eating. Carmen

hurried to put a plate in front of Elbow and serve up a concoction of taco chips, ground beef, onions and tomato sauce topped with cheese, then ran to get him a beer and waited impatiently for his reaction. He tasted it. She looked at him expectantly with big, puppy dog eyes.

The food was good, a little heavy on the onions maybe, but good. It went down well with the beer. Juan threw out a perfectly good cook. Elbow gave her a smile and said "Good. *Bueno*." She beamed.

Rosita allowed Pepito to wander around the table as they ate. Elbow kept a wary eye on his taco chips. The bird made several attempts but Elbow managed to discretely wave his fork in the winged marauder's direction to fend him off.

When he finished eating, Elbow sat back, digesting. "Carmen seems to be a good cook. Maybe the Flamingo would hire her. Their menu could use some spicing up. They're never too picky about where people come from or work papers."

Rosita smiled. "See, I tell you she good. You fix nice place for her."

"Okay, okay, tomorrow. Right now I'm pooped. I been working hard all afternoon on that bike. I got to get some shut-eye."

"Where she sleep tonight? You make her some bed or else she sleep in you bed!"

Red looked at him sympathetically. "Better do it. Rosita makes up her mind, it's hard to say no."

Elbow was too tired to argue. "Okay, I'll take the cart and see what I can find, but it won't be fancy."

Rosita smiled and scooped Pepito up from the table. The bird gave Elbow a screech and a couple of beak clicks as a parting gesture -probably birdspeak for "up yours".

Tired as he was, Elbow wheeled the grocery cart two blocks to the back of the exercise emporium. It was amazing what people threw away. On any given day there could be anything in the dumpster from slightly abused towels to broken furniture. Today he was in luck. They were tossing not one, but two, massage table cushions. Jackpot! There were also several large, cardboard, shipping boxes. He stuffed the cushions in the cart basket, folded the cardboard as best he could and balanced it on top.

It was slow going back to the warehouse with the awkward load and the wonky cart wheel bouncing over the cracked concrete alley surface. He took it slow. It was well after dark before he made it back to the warehouse and struggled through the steel door. Carmen was sitting at the card table, in the dark, waiting. She came to help.

It took Elbow an hour to put the long, narrow boxes together again with duct tape and then tape the two boxes together so the cushions could be placed high and dry on top, to make a somewhat comfy bed. He made motions with his hands that this was Carmen's bed and that she should go to sleep. She sat down on the construction and managed a small smile.

"Buenos nachos," Elbow said and headed for his own bed. While he was gone doing the dumpster run, Carmen had committed a 'clean and tidy' in his space. The floor was spotless. Clothes once piled in the corner were washed and hanging up to dry. Even some of the dirty windows were almost clean enough to see through.

Was nothing sacred? This was his private space. It may not have impressed the health department but it suited him just fine. A guy has a right to make his own space and no one should mess with it. Some things should be left just as they were.

It had been a long day. Up before dawn, locked in a car trunk, wrestling with the motorbike and then dealing with Carmen. It was

only eight-thirty p.m., but he was beat. He hoped Carmen hadn't messed with his bed too. He laid down on top of it, not even bothering to take off his shoes. Nothing like a fellow's own bed to make stinking bike tires, cheeky cockatoos and guys with guns go away. He slept.

• • • •

CARMEN SAT ON THE EDGE of the mattress-bed in the middle of the bare, cavernous warehouse, looking up at the rusty, metal girders hanging above her on the ceiling. The orange, safety light in the alley next door filtered through the broken windows to cast strange shadows that stretched across the floor to her feet.

She thought about her family and their small house behind her uncle's taqueria shop in Mexico. It was crowded. They all shared beds and food and were happy together. She remembered her mother's laugh. A tear made its way down her cheek. She tucked her knees up under her dress and laid down on the mattress. She curled up in a ball and cried softly in the dark.

She stayed there for about an hour until the pain of isolation became so great she could bear it no longer. She got up and quietly walked over to the plastic wall around Elbow's room to peek inside. He was asleep. She could hear him breathing in the dark. One silent step at a time, she crossed the floor to the edge of the bed. Elbow was sleeping on his side facing the windows. Carmen laid down gently next to him, snuggling up to his back. She smiled. It was just like home with the warmth of human company next to her. She sighed and closed her eyes.

• • • •

ELBOW SNORTED. STILL half asleep, he reached behind to scratch something that was poking him. He touched hair and a face.

"What the hell!" He sat up with a start. The bed became unbalanced, accidentally throwing Carmen to the floor.

"Ahhhooow," she cried out

Elbow stood up. "What the hell are you doing in my bed!"

Carmen started crying again.

"Are you hurt? Oh for heavens sake, you didn't fall far enough to get hurt. The bed is only twelve inches off the floor. What were you doing crawling around in my bed?"

Carmen sat on the floor speaking a stream of Spanish between sobs.

"Look, this is my bed, see! THAT is your bed." He pointed to the other side of the plastic. It only invoked more sobs.

Enough of Carmen already. Elbow needed to get away. Every time he turned around, there she was, into everything, his room, shopping, cooking, cleaning, the motorbike. Enough already! Time to go somewhere she couldn't. The Flaming Flamingo! A guy's refuge against the world with beer and other soothing beverages, the click of billiard balls and interesting female company. Sanctuary.

He looked at his watch. Eleven o'clock. The evening was just getting started at the Flamingo. He hurried out the warehouse door and down the alley to put quick distance between himself and the ever-present Carmen. It was a rapid turn at the corner and then fast steps down the street to the pink, dancing, flamingo legs over the door. He could hear the jukebox out on the street. There was a good crowd, just like every night.

"Elbow!" Ed, the bouncer shouted and grabbed Elbow's shirt to push him up against the wall. "I been lookin' for you."

"What's up, Ed, you're bending my lapels."

"Someone told me you got Brenda's motorbike."

"Yeah, sure, she told me to take it and fix it. It had that big snake wrapped around it, remember?"

"She says you took it."

"Sure, I took it. It was sitting on her front porch. The thing stunk to high heavens. Flies everywhere. Maybe she doesn't remember too clear. She had a fews beers that night, but she asked me to fix it."

Ed released his hold and let Elbow drop to the floor. "Hurry it up and get it back to her. She's pissed."

"Sure, sure. I finally got the snake off of it. I been working on the wheel. It was all bent up. These things take time."

"Soon, Snake-boy, you got that?"

"Got it. Soon." He made his escape and tried to move closer to the bar to order a beer. Man, Ed was wound up. Brenda must have given him an earful. Better steer clear of her for a while.

There was a scuffle at the door as a group of underage boys attempted to breach Ed's defense. Ed finally got the upper hand and started shouting. "Out! Everybody out! You don't get in here if you don't got a proper ID, especially you, little lady. This is a bar not a kindergarten. Out!"

For just a split second, Elbow thought he saw Carmen at the door. But no, that couldn't be. It must be because he was dehydrated. He took a sip of his beer, headed into the back room and surveyed the crowd.

"Elbow, how is my least favorite THIEF doing these days?"

"Brenda, I was just looking for you," he lied.

"Yeah, right."

"No, really. I fixed the bike. Ed said you were looking for it. You knew I took it, right?"

"Like hell!"

"It was on your front porch when I left. I almost tripped over it. Man, it was nasty. Stunk to high heavens with all that snake on it. It would have been a shame if your little dog got into it. Would have made her sick for a month. I had to wait until it all got gooey enough to pull the snake off. Then I had to straighten all the bent spokes and fit the wheel back on the bike."

"You better get it back to me quick."

"Sure, sure. Tomorrow. I'll even put gas in the tank. Okay?"

"Tomorrow, first thing!"

Elbow gave her one of his patented grins. "You know you never get up early after you been to the Flamingo the night before."

"Yeah, well, I'm cuttin' down on the beers, you know, all those calories."

"You never have to worry about that, Brenda. On you, curves look mighty fine." He looked her up and down. "Yes sir, mighty fine." Brenda was always a sucker for a compliment. Her anger melted. She tried not to smile. Elbow gave her another grin. He was home free. The night was looking more promising every minute. He spotted an empty booth and motioned her toward it. He ordered a couple more beers for good measure and they settled in.

The air in the back room of the Flamingo was getting hot and sticky so someone had the bright idea to open the back, exit door to let in some cooler, sticky air. Elbow laughed as he saw the group of teenage boys that had been turned away at the front door enter and slink along the wall near the pool tables. Music blasted from the jukebox. People were dancing. The familiar aroma of beer hung in the air.

He never noticed until it was too late. Somehow she had managed to sneak in behind the teenage boys and make her way invisibly across the crowded room and there she was, right behind his booth. Carmen's face popped up just inches away from him just as he was about to swallow some beer.

"Hell!" He yelled and choked with a coughing fit as the beer went down the wrong way. He struggled for breath. His face turned red. Carmen screamed. The room came to a standstill. The jukebox thumped on in the sudden silence. All eyes turned to look.

"What are you doing here?" Elbow finally managed to gasp out.

Carmen started wailing a stream of Spanish. People around them stared at Elbow in horror as she went on and on.

Brenda stood up and swung a fist at Elbow's head. "Pervert!" She yelled.

Then all hell broke loose. Whatever Carmen said set off a firestorm of anger from the crowd. Fists came at Elbow from all directions fueled by the abundance of beer, heat and Saturday night testosterone. He took refuge under the table where the number of hands grabbing at him was restricted by the sides of the booth.

The adolescent football team was up for a good fight and joined in just for the heck of it. Soon pool cues and billiard balls were flying through the air followed by beer bottles and an occasional chair. It

was a free-for-all. Old scores were settled, jealousies avenged, and heads thumped just because they were in the way.

Ed, the bouncer, entered the fray, trying to coral the worst offenders and thump a few heads himself, in an effort to minimize the damage to the Flamingo and save the furniture.

Elbow might have enjoyed the fight if he wasn't at the center of the commotion. He curled up in a ball under the table so there wouldn't be anything for anyone to hang onto to drag him out. Beer from the bottles on the table above him spilled over and cascaded down on the seats. He could still hear Carmen crying over the top of everything.

A billiard ball accidentally ricocheted into the kitchen knocking the cook's drink into the deep fryer, setting off a flash fire. The fire alarm went off.

Elbow heard sirens. The fire department and the police were about to break up the party. He had a sketchy history with the police department. Time to get out. As he crawled out from under the table and over the back of the booth, he found Carmen crouched next to the wall with her hands over her head. He grabbed her arm and pushed his way through the tangled crowd toward the back door, dragging her behind him. The door was already open and wiser patrons were headed for open air before the flying squad of police batons arrived.

In the parking lot, he pointed toward the warehouse. "Vamoose! Rosita, si?" Urging her to run.

He turned around just as a fist hit him squarely in the jaw. He fell against the side of a car, hitting his head on the side mirror on the way down. Brenda stood over him rubbing her sore knuckles. Carmen knelt down beside him trying to soothe the wound trickling blood down his forehead.

He grabbed Carmen's hand. "Vamoose. Police! Rosita!" He told her, hoping she would understand. Her eyes got wide and she suddenly seemed to comprehend. She hurried off down the street, melting into

the crowd gathering to look at the parade of police cars and fire trucks arriving in front of the Flamingo.

Elbow rubbed his jaw and looked up at Brenda. "What was that for?"

"You're a low life scum. Thats what that's for. I always knew you were bad news, but this is the lowest. I speak Spanish, you know. Sleeping with that poor little girl!"

"Wait, what? No, no, you've got the wrong end of the stick. Rosita told me to make her a bed, so I made her a bed. She didn't like it and I suddenly woke up with her curled up next to me in my bed. I didn't do anything! Sure I like the ladies, but she's just a kid. I'm not some sicko. That's just gross, Brenda. If you want to beat someone up, pound away on Juan. He brought her here from Mexico to marry her, then tossed her out. She doesn't have any ID. We were just trying to help her - Red and Rosita and me."

"Really? You're not just making that up?"

"No, really. If you don't believe me, ask Rosita."

"Oh, baby, I'm so sorry," Brenda caressed his chin.

Brenda's knuckle sandwich and the collision with the side mirror finally caught up with him. Elbow's eyes suddenly glazed over, his world turned black and he took a nose dive to the pavement.

Elbow had trouble focusing. There was an annoying beeping sound somewhere. Something was attached to his arm and he had a wide, cushy collar around his neck. Where the heck was he? This wasn't the warehouse. It was too clean. It wasn't Brenda's - no little dog in his face.

Hospital. He was in the hospital. The fight. Brenda's right hook. He reached up to his forehead and felt a bandage where he collided with something. He could tell there were stitches. That was going to leave a mark. One more scar.

There was a brisk knock at the door and a nurse entered the room to check on him. There was something about women in nurses' uniforms that always got Elbow's attention. This nurse was cute too.

"Well, how are you feeling, Mr. Smith? Have you been awake long?"

"No, I just woke up."

"Very good," she said and looked at her watch, then typed something on her little computer pad. Her name tag said ANNA. Elbow submitted willingly as she took his vital signs. He gave her a lazy smile and enjoyed watching her busy herself removing the IV and adjusting his pillows, making sure everything was checked off her list. She explained how he could order lunch, if he was hungry.

"What time is it, Anna," he asked.

"Two fifteen."

"Sunday?"

"No, Monday."

"They did all the tests this morning, Mr. Smith. The Doctor should be in to see you soon."

Good God, he had been out a whole day and a half. Brenda packed quite a wallop. She could take up professional, bare-knuckle boxing. And Carmen, did she make it back to the warehouse? At least by some

miracle he wasn't in jail. He gave Anna another smile as she left the room.

He fumbled through the hospital TV channels beyond information about heart attack warning signs and cholesterol diet hints. Not much sports coverage on Mondays so he settled for the news, and there it was, Miami's finest raiding the Flaming Flamingo. There were numerous cell phone pictures of the street clogged with ambulances, squad cars and people streaming out the front door, some in handcuffs.

There was also a quick shot of the interior. The Flaming Flamingo lived up to its name. The inside was trashed. Boy, when the Flamingo crowd gets heated up it really does a thorough job of it. The Flamingo wouldn't be open for a week or two while they shoveled out the glass and tried to find all the billiard balls. The kitchen looked like a total loss. Some reporter was yammering on about stricter laws to govern the bar industry.

Elbow ate a late lunch. The burger was unsalted, unadorned and pretty tasteless. Would it hurt to sneak a few grains of salt or a squirt of mustard on it or did everyone have to eat 'heart healthy'? Maybe it was a plot to empty the hospital as fast as they could so people would go home to eat real food.

There was a knock on the door. He hoped it was the cute Anna again. It was Brenda.

"Hi there, Elbow, how is it going?" she asked sweetly.

"Pretty good, Brenda, even though I didn't know what day it was 'cause I was in la-la land for a day and a half. You got some punch there."

"It wasn't me exactly. You fell against that car mirror. That did most of the damage."

"Sure, must have been the mirror," he said, but knew better. Brenda was being sweet, almost contrite. She even brought flowers. "How did I get here and not in jail? Everyone was hot be beat me up. What did Carmen say exactly that got everyone so riled up?"

"She said you pushed her out of bed onto the floor, and well, everyone assumed ... you know, ... that .. she and you were ... um .. They thought the worst."

"Yeah, I get the picture."

"I told the ambulance driver that some guys roughed you up, and the police checked your knuckles to see if you were fighting. Then they let them take you to the hospital."

"Thanks, Brenda."

"Yeah, sure. You're a lot of things, Elbow, but not so low as ... how old is she anyway?" She moved closer to the bed and stroked the bandage on his forehead. "I feel real bad about that nasty bump. Maybe I can make it up to you sometime."

"Yeah, we could make a night of it 'dancing' at the Flamingo, when they get it all cleaned up." He smiled. She smiled.

"I went to the warehouse and picked up the motorbike. I actually didn't believe you when you said it was all repaired. It must have been a big job. I even put gas in it and rode it here today. It works fine. Thanks, honey."

The door to the room opened and Rosita walked right in followed by a very shy Carmen. They brought the same kind of flowers as Brenda. It looked like the guy on the corner was having a special.

"Elbow, I come yesterday. You no awake. Carmen say she sorry. She say there big fight. Say you make her run away. You bad hurt? You don't look bad hurt. I fix."

Elbow held up his hand to stop whatever Rosita had in mind to 'fix'. "Thanks, Rosita, I think the hospital did a pretty good job. I'm glad Carmen made it back to the warehouse Okay."

"She scared like a rabbit. Almost not talk. I see Flamingo. Big mess."

There was another knock at the door. Wanda walked in with another matching bouquet of flowers. The guy on the corner was doing a land-office business.

"Well, this looks like a party! How are you doing, Elbow honey? They treatin' you right at the hospital? I saw the big thing at the Flamingo on the TV and there you were laying in the parking lot. For a moment I was scared you were dead or somethin', but they said there were no fatalities so I had Arnie track you down. Just came to see that one of our best customers was okay and everything." She smiled and leaned over to give him a kiss on the cheek.

"Hey, who are you?" Brenda said.

Elbow offered introductions. "Brenda, this is Wanda. She and Arnie run the bar and grill out on the river. And this is Rosita and Carmen.

Wanda smiled. "Pleased to meet y'all. We were worried about you, Elbow. Big Joe and Louisa heard about it too. They send their regards. Louisa, especially, said to say hi."

"Louisa! Who the hell is Louisa?" Brenda shouted.

Wanda smiled at Brenda. "Don't get all tied up in a knot, honey. Louisa is Big Joe's wife. She's kind of pretty in a skinny sort of way. They're regulars at our place, just like Elbow."

Brenda glared at Elbow. "What were you doing out in alligator country?"

Elbow started to sweat a little. "Fishing."

"Fishing? You never fished in your life," Brenda said. She was getting hot.

"Sure he goes fishing," Wanda piped up. "He even rescued Big Joe's boat. That's how he got that nasty cut on his knee. I helped him bandage it up, didn't I, sugar?" She reached out on top of the hospital sheet and patted his knee with her long, red fingernails.

"Now just a minute, don't you go playing patty-cake with his knee."

"I'm just bein' friendly like."

The door banged open. A figure that took up most of the door frame came in and looked around. Elbow groaned. It was the muscle suit. The suit nodded toward the door and Abba entered carrying a bunch of roses. She was dressed in a baby blue, silk outfit that set off her silver hair to perfection. They all turned to stare at her. She took one glance around the room and headed straight for Elbow, pushing Brenda out of the way.

"Well, Mr. 'El Beau,' I wondered what happened to you. Seems like you prefer beer and brawling in bars rather than margaritas on the patio. The TV shots of you weren't exactly flattering. You left without saying goodbye."

"If I told you what happened, you might not believe me," Elbow said, trying to control his voice.

"Try me."

"Get rid of 'Bruno' here and I will."

Abba gave the suit a nod to send him out into the hall. The man started to leave and turned to give Elbow a warning look before lumbering out the door.

"It was like this, Abba ..."

Brenda put her hands on her hips. "Abba? First Carmen and Rosita, then Wanda, Louisa and now Abba! Good God, how many more women are going to march in here? You are one sleazy operator, Elbow. And you, fancy pants Abba, who the hell are you?"

Abba looked Brenda up and down, brushed Brenda's flowers off the night stand and turned back to Elbow.

Brenda was incensed. "Why you snobby little bitch!" She grabbed Abba's roses and threw them up in the air. Abba snatched Wanda's bouquet and stuffed it in Brenda's face. After that it was everyone for themselves. When Wanda and Rosita got into the action, fists flew, hair got pulled, and shins kicked.

Elbow tried to stay out of the way. He stood up on the bed yelling for everyone to remain calm. When the behemoth bodyguard stepped in, Elbow decided it was time to be somewhere else. Someone shoved the bed and he headed for the closet to get his clothes. It was a little hard getting dressed while dodging flower stems and swinging fists but he managed to slip into his jeans and find his shoes. At the last second he grabbed his tee shirt and stuffed it in his pocket. He made it to the door before a lampshade hit the wall next to him. Wanda screamed and connected with Brenda's chin. Rosita climbed up the muscle suit's back and bit his ear. If anyone could bring the muscle suit down, it was Rosita. Elbow hoped she didn't travel with her gun.

Elbow escaped into the hall. He tried to look casual and inconspicuous. limping his way to the stairs as he put on his shoes. Hospital staff was already on alert, running toward the room to quell the riot. Elbow checked his back pocket for his wallet. It was still there. He felt the lump in his shoe where the rest of his stash was stored. All essentials were accounted for.

On the stairs, he took off the spongy neck brace and hung it on the railing. He struggled to remove the hospital gown. It was still tied tightly behind his neck. To hell with it. He tucked it randomly in his jeans. He was in a hurry. At the bottom of the stairs he stumbled out the emergency exit door into the parking lot.

Transportation. He needed wheels. Then he spotted it - Brenda's motorbike parked in the second row. It wouldn't make any difference if he took the bike to make a quick getaway. Brenda was going to be mad as hell anyway. He knew the bike inside and out. Starting it without the key only took two minutes. He could hear sirens. They had sent for reinforcements. Definitely time to go.

As squad cars hit the front entrance, Elbow motored out the rear exit. Traffic was heading south so he went with the flow. He had to think. The warehouse and the Flamingo might not be the best place to hide out right now. Time to make a new plan. He had money in his pocket. He could go anywhere. South was a good direction, new territory, a fresh start.

He wound his way through Miami proper and along the stretch of hotels and beaches where Northern tourists were frying in the sun. Then he saw the sign, KEY WEST - KEEP LEFT. It was as good a place as any for an irregular, free spirited soul like himself. He turned with traffic and soon was speeding along over a ribbon of concrete stretched out over azure blue water.

With the wind blowing in his hair and the sun sparkling on the water, he felt free. No brawling women. No damn cockatoo and no grimy warehouse. No cares. La dolce vita.

He was no longer driving through congested Miami at twenty mies an hour. At sixty, the wind began to whip the sides of the hospital gown against his sides and shoulders. He struggled to untie it again with one hand, the other hand steering the bike. The knot wouldn't budge. He slipped this arms out of the sleeves one at a time and turned the whole gown around to the back. With the cape flapping wildly behind him he looked like a hospital version of superman. The wind pulled at the cape and the string-like tie began to strangle him.

The Keys Causeway is one of those places where you don't pause to scratch your nose or admire the scenery. If there is a problem, you keep your eyes glued to the road and pray for an island or one of those small, pullout, rest stop bulges in the pavement to appear soon. About a mile ahead he could see one approaching. The car behind him was closing fast. Elbow slowed down but the car didn't. At the last second, Elbow pulled the motorbike into the rest stop. There was a screeching of brakes and a few angry hand gestures from the car as it roared past and got back up to speed.

The quick turn and sliding stop were too much for the repaired wheel spokes. The wheel bent every which way and collapsed under him as the bike skidded to a stop against the side railing. Elbow sat there for a moment trying to comprehend what just happened as parts of the bike lay scattered around him. One minute he was whizzing along free as a bird and the next he's sitting inches from the pavement on a crumpled chunk of nothing.

He stood up and did a personal inventory. Two arms, two legs still attached. Nothing was bleeding. He looked at the bike. It was now scrap metal. He looked up at the sky. "WHY ME?" He yelled at the gods.

He took his anger out on the annoying hospital gown, tearing the fabric away from the stubborn tie around his neck. He matted it up into a ball and tossed it over the railing into the Gulf of Mexico. He kicked the offending bike for good measure. Next, he picked up what was left of the bike and heaved it over the edge too. It made a satisfying splash, then sank up to the gas tank with the front wheel sticking out of the water like some sort of final salute. "Take that you miserable 'snake bike!'" He yelled into the wind.

His satisfaction was short lived. He suddenly realized he was in the middle of nowhere, surrounded by water, miles from land. Walking anywhere along the causeway was deadly and definitely frowned upon. Nothing for it but to try to thumb a ride.

He retrieved his shirt from his back pocket and put it on to make himself more presentable, then walked up a bit against traffic to sit on the railing to hang out his thumb. The first ten cars whizzed by without even looking. There was a lull in traffic. Then he saw it coming toward him, a convertible, all white and shiny against the blue sky and ocean with a blond at the wheel. He stood up on the concrete next to the railing, gave her a thumb and one of his grins. The car slowed down and pulled over in the rest area. Elbow ran to catch up.

"Hi, you going somewhere?" The blond asked.

"Yeah, anywhere but the middle of the ocean," he said and grinned.

She smiled back. "Hop in. We can't leave you standing out here. I'm headed to Key West."

"Thanks, that's where I'm headed too." He opened the door and slid in.

She checked for traffic behind her and pulled out onto the highway. The sun was making its late afternoon descent into the western horizon. The moon was just rising over the water in the East. The air was warm. Elbow settled back into the comfy seat and admired his companion. She had all the right attributes in all the right places. She wore a sleeveless pink top and short shorts. Her pink sunglasses had little rhinestones in the corners. She looked at him and gave him another pretty smile. Yes sir, things were looking better every minute. The night stretched before him like in a dream. What could go wrong?

END

Don't miss out!

Visit the website below and you can sign up to receive emails whenever Kay Wahlgren publishes a new book. There's no charge and no obligation.

https://books2read.com/r/B-A-YDWU-LXQAC

BOOKS 2 READ

Connecting independent readers to independent writers.